The Gift of Fire

ALSO BY WALTER MOSLEY

WALTER MOSLEY

CROSSTOWN TO OBLIVION

The Gift of Fire

TOR®

A TOM DOHERTY ASSOCIATES BOOK • NEW YORK

THE GIFT OF FIRE / ON THE HEAD OF A PIN

Copyright © 2012 by Walter Mosley

Design by Mary A. Wirth

A Tor Book
Published by Tom Doherty Associates, LLC
175 Fifth Avenue
New York, NY 10010

www.tor-forge.com

Tor® is a registered trademark of Tom Doherty Associates, LLC.

Library of Congress Cataloging-in-Publication Data

Mosley, Walter.
    The gift of fire ; On the head of a pin : two short novels from crosstown to oblivion / Walter Mosley.—1st ed.
        p. cm.
    ISBN 978-0-7653-3008-6 (hardcover)
    ISBN 978-1-4299-8576-5 (e-book)
    I. Mosley, Walter. On the head of a pin.   II. Title.   III. Title: On the head of a pin.
    PS3563.O88456G54 2012
    813'.54—dc23

                                                                    2012001827

First Edition: May 2012

Printed in the United States of America

0 9 8 7 6 5 4 3 2 1

In honor of PKD

The Gift of Fire

PART ONE

PROLOGUE

THE EAGLE HAD already gouged out his belly when lightning struck metal at early dawn and Prometheus—golden-
skinned, curly-haired, brown-eyed son of the Mediterranean
Spirit—slipped his chains, gathered his intestines up in his
left hand, and made his way clambering down the mountain path; that long forgotten trail that once connected
Gods and Men . . . and Titans. Behind him he could hear
the ravenous eagle crying out for blood. Every day for three
thousand years the hungry bird ate his liver, leaving him at
night so that the organs and flesh and broken bones grew
and knit back together befitting his immortal nature. In
spring the hideous fowl brought his chicks to peck and pull
at the cords of skin and meat. Every bite and tug sent agony
through the beautiful Titan's frame, racking him in agony,
leaving him spent and yet unable to die.

Crying, he ran down in the shadow of overhanging rocks
and trees. He ran, muttering to himself, "I have not yet fin-
ished. The gift of the gods is incomplete."

His father, Iapetus, or his mother, Clymene, of the ocean, if they had seen their son, would have told him to forget his quest, to go to some peaceful place, maybe the Elysian Fields, and hide from the vengeance of the gods. Hiding was the only escape. Even his brother Atlas did not have the strength to defy Zeus and his heavenly host.

Prometheus sorely missed his mother and brother, his father and other siblings, but he had gone mad chained to that rock, tortured by the evil bird and the God King's curse.

He wanted to hide, to be soothed from the suffering that had been brought down upon him. But he could not forget the job left undone: his misery and Man's.

"Run away," he said to himself. "Hide down under the earth where Pluto might protect you. Dive down under the ocean of the gods and beg Neptune to hide you.

"No," he said then. "I will not cower and beg as I have done for all these centuries. I will not bend my knee, lower my head, or forget my mission. May the gods choke on the caprice of their actions, may they die upon their hallowed mount forgotten in the minds of their minions."

And while the eagle wheeled in the sky the diminished Titan made his way under shadow of leaf and cover of night until he was away from the land of the gods, arriving where everything is mortal and anyone, even a god, can die.

HE FOUND HIMSELF upon a hilltop. To his right rolled the waves of a great ocean and to his left sprawled a mortal city with its temporary structures and its people who lived and died without suspicion of the knowledge that they partially comprehended but never knew. The smell of their smoke and feces filled his nostrils and burned his eyes. It was ever this way when gods and Titans mingled among humans. Mortals were like animals to those of the higher planes, snuffling and snorting and spraying urine to mark their domain.

Los Angeles was to Prometheus like a dung hill is to a swan—dirty and diseased, stinking of mortality—and yet these were the fallow grounds for the possibility of life.

ONE

His clothes were bloody and dirty from talon and beak and the mad dash from heaven. No one would seek him on earth because there was no godhood here. Zeus could die as any housefly or beached mackerel or whale. Ares, god of war, could fall on a mortal battlefield. There was no reincarnation, no rising from the dead for the old gods. Time on earth was immutable and the stench was what life had to have before it could ascend . . .

"Hey, you," a man's voice called. The language was strange to the Titan but its meaning was clear.

The man who addressed him was in a horseless carriage that smelled sour and poisonous. The metal vehicle was black and white while the uniforms that both men wore were black alone.

"Yes?" Prometheus replied in the old tongue.

The soldiers, or maybe city guardsmen, climbed out of thick metal doors grasping long black sticks.

"You drunk, pal?" one of them said.

Gazing into the fire of the pale-skinned man's mind the immortal saw the word for the grape and smiled. He nodded thinking that maybe they were offering him a bladder for drink.

"What happened to your clothes, buddy?" the other man, *police*man, asked.

Looking down Prometheus saw that his tunic, hand sewn by his mother, was tattered, torn, and filthy. His manhood showed through the tears and the little men of earth seemed to be made shy by this.

"I bring you the gift of fire," he said, still speaking the old tongue, the language of sand and sea.

"Cover yourself up," the pale-skinned policeman on the left commanded.

Reaching into his soul with his mind as a mortal man might open his purse, Prometheus found the Second Fire, the flame that would connect the human mind with the realm above. He found the small, flickering, opalescent thing, tiny as a blade of grass that stood alone on a vast and desolate plane that had been a forest—now sundered and razed. This tiny fire was not matter or heat or anything that human senses had ever perceived. It was the fount of godly thought and not even many Olympians knew of it.

The flame was small and weak, leaping from the scorched firmament so as not to be doused by the devastation.

It was almost dead. All those years chained and tortured

were designed to completely destroy the Titan Prometheus, not only his life but his ability to know.

The policemen had flanked him but the seven-foot giant of Mediterranean and African perfection did not heed their strange words. Instead he climbed into himself, in his mind, and hunkered down around the last wavering glimmer of what made him who he was and what he was. He sang the Psalm of Awakening taught to him by Chronos near the River Styx in his youth. It was the story of a ram named Iricles who, each day, climbed up from the depths of the world with a bell tied to his tail. The tinkling sound of the tin bell was what the sun needed to find her way back into the sky.

It was a deadly song. When the gods sang they put their souls into the music and the words. Lovers had died from godly music; wars had been waged for a hundred years over the immortal use of pipe and poem. And here on earth Prometheus risked the final death by singing to the last shimmering vestige of his godhood.

He was gone from the external world singing, exhorting the Gift to survive. He didn't feel the policemen grapple him, trying to wrestle him to the ground. He didn't hear their threats or feel the blows of their nightsticks. The song of Chronos was in him now. Inside his soul was a world that no human could comprehend—not yet. He squatted down on a plane made desolate by centuries of suffering at the hands of the gods. All that was left was this tiny sparkle like the last reflection of the sun before nightfall on one small rise in the sea.

As the policemen beat his body to the ground—he sang.

As the sun in his mind seemed to be setting into a final night—he sang. And somewhere, impossibly far from Sunset Boulevard, a forest suddenly surged into being. Ancient trees and bold stags, great flat-faced bears and birds who took up the ancient Titan song were alive again. The Second Fire loomed in the air above the weary god's head. It turned slowly, its flames like the facets of a delicate jewel eluding the eye, exulting in the place it held.

Prometheus opened his eyes and rose from the ground, throwing the men off of him like children. They brought out metal weapons from holsters in their belts.

"On your knees!" the brown-skinned policeman commanded.

"I bring you the second gift," Prometheus said now in the English tongue.

"Down on your knees!" the pale-skinned man screamed.

They were frightened of his strength. It occurred to Prometheus that it had been many thousands of years since men had met their dreams.

At another time he would have killed these simple foot soldiers for the disrespect they showed him. He would have torn off their heads and roasted their flesh, raped their women and enslaved their children and their children's children. He would have burned down their houses and filled an oaken tub with their blood. . . . But those days were gone. When Prometheus had given the First Flame to mankind he gave up the raging lust of godhood. He'd made men into something more even if they only dimly understood their metamorphosis.

Instead of destruction the immortal opened his arms

wide. He was intent upon bestowing the gift of his inner fire onto mankind. These men would be the kindling and soon, within a decade, the world of humanity would be aflame with awareness.

Reaching into himself again Prometheus sought the memory of Gaea's Song of Sharing. It was a potent song from deep in the earth, a music that could shake the soul out of a king. There were no words to this music, no instrument other than the voice of a god that could embody the melody.

Prometheus located the place where this song lived in his soul, but his torture, the stench of humanity, the Psalm of Awakening, and the beating he had taken were too much for him. He staggered forward and fell to the ground and for the first time in three thousand years Prometheus slept without pain or fear of the dawn.

TWO

THE STENCH BROUGHT him back to consciousness. It was a smell so foul that the Titan's dreaming mind feared that he had somehow awakened in the darker half of Pluto's realm. He jumped to his feet and saw that he was in a cage with a dozen mortal men. One of these was vomiting on the floor, another was sitting on a metal toilet defecating and groaning as if the act might kill him.

The smell was noxious enough to make a Titan cry.

"What the fuck kinda niggah is you, man?" someone asked.

It was a black-skinned man who addressed him. A man with beautiful dark eyes and a ravaged face. He was dying. Prometheus could see this clearly.

"I am . . ." Prometheus's mind zipped into the ether, looking for a name that would somehow hold a meaning for him.

"Prospect," he said. "Foreman Prospect."

The Titan held out his hand to the man.

"You one big mothahfuckah," the scrawny black man said. "I give ya that much."

Prometheus perceived the wily look in his new friend's eye. There was something he wanted.

"How are you called?" the Olympian asked.

"Nosome is the moniker my mama hung me wit'. Ain't no beautiful name, but you won't find nobody wit' the same handle an' you won't find nobody else like me."

Prometheus smiled at his new friend as they clasped hands.

Newly named Foreman Prospect saw that he was now clad in a shirt and pants that were a soft gray color. There was no flair or meaning to the clothes, no insignia or ranking. He wondered if the humans meant to make him their slave.

"I am new here, Sir Nosome," he said. "I will need somebody to show me around the city."

"I'm yo' man, Brother Prospect. I know this gottdamned city like the back a my mothahfuckin' hand. But they gonna let me out soon. I tell you what though, I sleep all ovah the place but I hang out at Crenshaw and Thirty-fifth. You come out there any day from sunup to sundown an' I'll be there."

The stench of the world did not diminish the friendship and the resolve in the dying man's eyes. Prometheus wondered if this old, diseased frame could take his gift of fire. So intent was he on this consideration he didn't notice the young men that approached him from the other side of the cage.

"What you got, man?" a well-muscled black man asked.

"The gift of fire," Prometheus responded without hesitation.

The man was surrounded by other dark-skinned young men. Some had gold on their teeth. All were tattooed with arcane symbols, sigils, and signs.

"What the fuck you say, man?"

The second fire was now strong in the meta-god's soul. He reached out to bestow his treasure. Standing at least a head over the young leader Prometheus touched his bare neck with a finger.

For an instant the young man looked up in shock and surprise . . . then his eyes went white; he screamed and flung himself backward hitting two of his four followers, throwing them to the ground.

The man ran for the bars of the cell. When his friends tried to stop him he fought like some feral beast trapped and cornered. Blood and heavy blows attended the battle.

"What's wrong with him?" Nosome asked. He had moved behind his tall friend.

"His soul has been tortured," Foreman Prospect replied.

"Huh?"

"I have seen it before, in myself."

The battle continued. Now the men were fighting back, still surprised by their leader's sudden betrayal.

A bell sounded somewhere and uniformed guards came running down the slender, metal-floored corridor that separated the cages. Looking up through the metal grids Prometheus could see that this was a tower of caged men. Floor after floor separated by crisscrossed steel grating.

"Are we under attack?" he asked Nosome.

The elder man took the Ancient by the arm, led him to a cot, and made him sit down.

"They comin' to break up the fight," Nosome said. "If you don't wanna get beat no mo' an' you wanna get outta here 'fore you grow a full beard then just sit wit' yo' hands on yo' knees and let them do they job."

Prometheus could hear the honesty in Nosome's words and so he sat down and watched as a dozen men in black uniform descended on the fighting friends. The beating was harsh but not overly brutal in Olympian eyes. They used sticks and fists to subdue the men. They bound the one who had been touched by fire. He screamed and struggled.

"Let me outta here!" he shouted staring at Prometheus. "Help me!"

Nosome and his new friend Foreman Prospect sat plainfaced, hands upon their knees. The guards seemed to recognize and accept this behavior. They took the man away leaving the stink of the sweat and bowel movements, the scent of blood-stained metal and the fetid breath of slaves.

THREE

"NOSOME BLANE," a man called.

"Yessir," Prometheus's first friend in three thousand years replied in military cadence.

"You're outta here," the man said.

"What about my friend?" Nosome said. "What about Mr. Prospect?"

"Worry about yourself, wino," the policeman said. He was pink-skinned and paunchy, wearing spectacles but still squinting to make out the words written on a paper that was fastened to a thin fake-wood plank. "Take your skinny ass outta there before I haul you up in front'a the judge."

Fear shot through Nosome's weak frame. Prometheus could see it as a delicate network of iridescent blue and red lights flashing in the man's chest and head. But still Nosome hesitated.

"Don't give 'em no trouble, Prospect. I can tell you ain't used to this shit. Just tell the man what he wanna hear and don't lie 'bout nuthin' he could catch you up on."

"Are you coming?" the police warden said.

"They ain't nuthin', man," Nosome hissed. "Don't let 'em get to ya like they did with Luther."

"All right," the spectacled cop said. He started to move away from the door.

"I'm comin'," Nosome cried. "I'm comin'."

The frightened man ran to the cage door and went out, glancing at Foreman Prospect as he went.

The Greek deity smiled at his friend. He knew the love of this man in the few short hours that they had shared, imprisoned in a hell worthy of Pluto.

The man Nosome spoke of, Luther Unty, had been taken away and he did not return. Nosome thought Luther had broken under the pressure of having been in prison.

"Young men think they all strong an' shit," Nosome confided in his new friend, "but they don't know how to bend in a storm. They don't know how to grow out between the bars, and the laws and the men come down on 'em like boulders in a rockslide. They think 'cause they strong that they ain't nobody evah been stronger, but one day they learn—an' it's a terrible lesson, too."

Prometheus knew that it was his second gift of fire that had driven the, what Nosome called a, gangbanger insane. The firmament in the man's soul had rotted in a world where the purity of the first fire had been tainted and diminished. It was the celestial's touch that had brought to the surface the wreckage of Luther Unty's mind.

But Nosome's words went deeper. Prometheus was also once strong and sure, a fool. He had stood up against the gods and had paid a price as dear as Unty had. He had gone mad and rushed from heaven into the mortal realm where he could perish. He had almost lost the fount of godhood.

And so, hours after Nosome was gone, when the man with the flat board came and said, "You, you gotta name yet?"

"Foreman Prospect," Prometheus proclaimed in a voice that came from deep inside his mind and soul.

The officer peered up over his glasses as if he had heard something unexpected.

"What?"

"Foreman Prospect . . . from Kansas."

The strange look from the bureaucrat didn't surprise Prometheus. He had gone deep into his past, before the time of his imprisonment by Zeus and daily evisceration; back to a time when the deity named Logos took on physical form, that of a beautiful child, and led young Prometheus away from Olympus and everything he knew.

"WHERE ARE WE GOING?" the young immortal asked five thousand years ago.

"To the lands of our origins," the black-haired and ancient child replied.

And as he spoke they found themselves on a green-glass firmament suspended in a forever sky of blue and white.

"This is Heliopolis," Logos announced, "the land where our mind was engendered."

"There was something before us?" Prometheus asked.

"And before that," Logos said, and then he giggled. "Come on."

The waif child of the One Word ran down a street peopled with dark-skinned giants who moved with extraordinary dignity and grace. Prometheus desired to stop and study these new, strange, unexpected beings, but he didn't want to lose sight of Logos.

The child was running down a dark alley that was filthy, filled with beggars and bad smells. As Prometheus followed dark hands reached out to him for food or silver or maybe just the touch of vitality. But Prometheus didn't let anyone delay or even lay a single finger on him. He ran a zigzag path following the blue toga of Logos.

But the personification of The Word was fleet, unhindered by the awareness of the paupers or physical limits of any type. Soon he had disappeared and more and more the dark-skinned beggars crowded around trying to grab hold of the Hellenic deity.

Prometheus pushed their hands away, ducked and dodged and leaped over them. He realized that the giants he'd seen before had become these creatures and, further, he was in some way the cause of their plight.

As soon as this thought went through his mind young Prometheus found himself delivered from the grasping, silent hands and, though still in darkness, he stood before a muslin-bound doorway through which only the slightest hint of light escaped.

"Do not mourn the passing of the gods," Logos said then. He was standing next to him smiling.

"But they have been brought low and I fear that it is my fault," young Prometheus said.

"Is fire the fault of lightning or fear the fault of the lion?"

Logos asked. "But worry not, the flames burn themselves out and the fang breaks with age."

With these words the embodied concept pulled back the cloth door and a light ten times brighter than Apollo's shone, blinding the young Olympian.

"Welcome, Prometheus the destroyer," an old woman's voice groaned. "Your coming was prophesized before there were Titans or Gods."

She was very old, wrapped in rags, but her solar eyes were those of immortal ken. She smiled and the light that filled the room seemed to soak into her body, making her strong again, vital and young.

Now a beautiful woman of great height and profound dignity stood over him. Her skin was dark and her cheekbones high.

Prometheus noticed that Logos had crouched down, head bowed. Falling upon one knee Prometheus felt right, as if for the first time he was in perfect syncopation with the meaning of his existence.

"I am Ma'at," the goddess announced. "I am truth in all of its chaos and form. For ten thousand years in a mortal mind I was and still am the path that leaves and arrives at the same place . . . forever."

"Why have I been brought here, Goddess?" the young spirit of knowledge asked. His head was bowed out of respect, but also because to look upon Ma'at's brightness was painful. Her visage held the pain of oblivion: a cavern so deep that even the great stone giants of the lower realms would not have been able to scale it.

"Somewhere," she said, "between here and the beginning,

I gave birth to Logos and then died. He is not truth but a claim of being. I no longer exist, however my Word lives on."

Prometheus considered what she said but he did not understand.

"When you return to the world of your upbringing remember me," Ma'at said, "and remember that when you know a thing that is fitting you must not hold back."

Prometheus closed his eyes, shut them tight trying to understand the words without being distracted by painful light. He was to be the first and last of the embodied immortals to know the truth and the lie.

And when he opened his eyes he was sitting in the middle of a field of newly planted wheat on earth. The wind was blowing through his hair and Logos had disappeared into the world of Man. The child god smiled, knowing his destiny because of a Truth that came in a dream.

FOUR

"HE CALLS HIMSELF Foreman Prospect," someone was saying.

Prometheus opened his eyes and saw that he was standing behind a short wooden gate and looked down upon by a woman wearing a black robe with a white collar.

". . . but he doesn't have any identification," the man who was speaking continued.

Self-named Prospect could see that the middle-aged woman, his judge, found him fair. He could see in her eyes yellow sparks of passion that brought surprise to her face. How long had it been since this handsome, brown-skinned woman had felt her loins react to a man like she was a maiden.

"What is your name?" she asked.

"Foreman Prospect . . . from Kansas City, Kansas," he said, repeating words that he had practiced with Nosome Blane.

"And where do you live, Mr. Prospect?" the judge asked, her eyes reflecting the confusion in her fast blood.

"A small blue house at the corner of Crenshaw and Thirty-fifth, Your Honor," Prometheus replied. Words were coming to him through the air. Somewhere he could hear the child Logos laughing. "I don't know the number because I have only just made, um, arrangements to live there. My friend, Nosome Blane, is the landlord."

"And why don't you have identification?" the judge asked, trying not to smile coyly.

"I lost whatever I had, Your Honor. I've been away and haven't needed a passage stone."

"Your Honor," the man standing next to the beautiful giant complained.

This man was also dark-skinned, though not so much as the woman judge. He seemed pained that Foreman was getting such mild treatment.

"Yes, Mr. Gordon?"

"This man could be an illegal alien for all we know. We should at least make Homeland Security aware of him."

"He looks like an American," the judge (her nameplate read Bohem) said. "He talks like an American."

"He was found walking half-naked down Sunset Boulevard," the younger Gordon replied. "He resisted arrest. Officer Tynan sprained his ankle."

"Mr. Prospect?" the judge asked solicitously.

"I haven't moved into my house yet, Judge Bohem. And living next to this big rock I guess my clothes . . . you know."

"And your resisting arrest?"

"I have no excuse," Prometheus said. "I was confused I guess."

"More like high," Prosecutor Gordon complained.

"You have his Breathalyzer results?" Anna Bohem asked.

"No, ma'am. After the struggle the officers were lucky to get this big fella into their vehicle."

"It says in the arrest record that Mr. Prospect was rendered unconscious," the judge read, momentarily bringing reading glasses to her eyes.

"They were fighting for their lives, ma'am."

"There's no record of either officer being hospitalized."

"This man," Gordon said, "is seven feet tall and strong."

"Mr. Prospect," Judge Bohem said.

"Yes, Your Honor."

"I am inclined to let you go home, but I expect you to return to my offices with papers proving your identity."

"Your Honor," Gordon complained. "I must object."

"Mr. Gordon, this is my courtroom, is it not?"

"Yes, ma'am."

"Bailiff," the judge said then.

"Your Honor," an older, parchment-colored man said. He stood up from a chair against the far right wall.

"Find some suitable clothes for the defendant and send him on his way. Make sure that he has the information to get in touch with me . . . to prove his citizenship. Is that satisfactory, Mr. Gordon?"

The prosecutor mumbled something and Foreman Prospect was hustled from the court.

———

AFTER THE HEARING Prometheus was shuttled from room to room. He was given clothes that were both too large and too small for his perfect frame. His blue jean pants needed a belt but didn't go down as far as his ankles. His red checkered shirt was tight across his chest but loose around the middle. The shoes they gave him were rubber sandals without heels but he didn't care.

He was asked to write his name and address on a long form that had much tiny writing upon it. Using the spirit of Ma'at he produced what he meant and what they would believe. Later the ancient Greek symbols would be indecipherable, but at that moment he was Foreman Prospect from the blue house at Thirty-fifth and Crenshaw.

After two hours of processing, John Bolt, the ancient bailiff, handed the young giant two bills and said, "The judge wanted you to have this forty dollars. You don't have to sign for it."

"How do I get to Thirty-fifth and Crenshaw from here?" Prometheus asked.

"Bus right out in front of the court building."

EITHER IT WAS HIS SIZE or fair looks, or maybe it was his innocence that carried him to the street and to the door of the right bus. People showed him the way, forgave him for not having a pass or the right change, made room for him and chatted with him.

Gazing at them, Foreman Prospect, recently the prisoner

of Olympus, saw into their souls. He perceived that though these people were kind and helpful they all had the flaw of impoverished spirit; most, if not all, of them would go mad if he bestowed the Gift upon them.

Mankind, he could see, had fallen on hard times much as he had. The suffering he endured for sharing the first gift had also been visited upon Man. They had been driven mad for suspecting a higher realm but being forever barred from knowing it.

FIVE

AT 3:17 THAT AFTERNOON the Titan walked into an empty lot where five men were sitting in a circle, passing around a glass jug of wine. Some sat on sad discarded chairs and others on crates. One man was squatting down. This last one was laughing, telling a tale about a narrow escape.

Their smell was pungent and strong but Prometheus had been growing accustomed to the scents of Man. He walked up to the circle of small black men looking among them for his friend.

"Have any of you seen Nosome Blane?" he asked.

The men were mostly older, except for one who looked to the Titan to be barely out of his youth. They were all dark-skinned and sorely lacking in the place where there should have been the vitality of fire.

"What's wrong wit' yo' eyes?" asked a man who wore a soiled, light blue suit.

In the daylight Prometheus's eyes took on the aspect of the moon. At night, under the stars, his orbs blazed like fire.

"You got cataracts or sumpin'?" the blue-suited man continued.

"I am looking for Nosome Blane."

"What for?" a different man asked. This one was fat and angry. Prometheus could see the rage as dark snakes orbiting above his head.

"I owe him this." Prometheus held out the two twenty-dollar bills that the bailiff had given him.

The fat man stood up quickly and reached for the money but the Titan lifted his hand above his head, far out of the reach of anyone there.

"You play b-ball?" the young man asked. " 'Cause if you do we could make that cash in yo hand into some real money."

"I'm looking for Nosome," Prometheus repeated. "I will give him this cash."

"He was here," a fourth man said. He was small, an old man wearing simple clothes. His buttonless shirt and trousers were black and his shoes were bright red, made from fabric and not hide.

Prometheus instantly liked this man. He was a leader not out of pride or ambition but just because it was his duty.

"What you want with him?" the leader asked.

"My name is Foreman Prospect," Prometheus said. "I met Nosome last night in jail."

"I'm Willy," the leader said. "If you was in jail then how did he lend you anything?"

"I owe him. He helped me and I promised him this."

"What's wit' yo eyes, man?" Willy asked.

THE GIFT OF FIRE

"I'm from the islands," the Titan said.

"Jamaica?"

"Far from here."

Willy stared at the tall stranger with intention. The fires still burned in this man, that was why others followed him. But he was sick and his heart was weak. He could be ignited by the Gift, but the ecstasy of enlightenment would also kill him.

"Nosome come back from the drunk tank this mornin'," Willy said in measured tones. "But had a attack an' the social services van come an' took him home."

"Mothahfuckahs shoulda took him to the hospital," the angry fat man spat. "It's they job to take him to the emergency room, but the damn doctors pay the drivers off so that they don't have to see about us."

Prometheus saw now why the fat man had snakes swimming around his mind. The world had cheated him, had cheated his father and his father's father and his father before him.

"Where does Nosome live?" the Titan asked, knowing that the only cure for these men was the proper vessel for the Ascendant Flame.

"Walk that way for eight, nine miles and when you get to one hundred and four turn right," Willy said. "After a block or two there's gonna be a house with a blue roof and brick façade, that's Nosome's sister's place. That's where they took him an' you know she wouldn't nevah turn her big brother away."

Prometheus smiled at Willy. He put every ounce of his titanic will into the gratitude he felt. For a moment the dark-faced, soon-to-be-dead leader glared, but then his own smile broke through. It wasn't the gift of flame that the Titan bestowed, but it was an offer of respect for a man who had been set aside and forgotten even though every day of his life had been dedicated to leading others out from danger and loss.

THE WALK WAS FILLED with momentary meetings, stares, and strange sights. Foreman Prospect, his rubber flip-flops slapping against his soles, walked among people both black and brown. He heard them and smelled them and felt their joys and despair. The air was laced with toxic gasses similar to those that rose from Vulcan's noxious smithy. The music from passing cars was primal—filled with both desire and rage.

People asked him if he was white, if he was a basketball player. One young woman offered to take him home. But newly christened Foreman Prospect felt that he had not one moment to waste in his brief time among mortals. He could see, more and more clearly, the urgency of his mission with each step on the paved streets.

When he was last on earth humans built great and small mausoleums to bury their dead, ushering them from this world to the next. Now the entire race built a Hades to live in, a kind of madhouse of poisons, screaming machines, and lies.

As he was eviscerated so had been the human race. Their population was swollen like ants on a stag's corpse, but in all their multiplication they had lost sight of their singular beauty, of their individual souls. They were dying and they were dead staggering under the weight of futile labors. They were inebriated and fat, unloved and unloving. Children had the eyes of old women and their bodies were riddled with disease.

Somehow gods and men had turned their backs on each other. The divinity in man had aged and was dying. The empathy of the immortal realm had dried up.

Prometheus felt that he was the last connecting tissue between what was and what might be. Knowing the Fire that burns on Fire he understood that gods and men were interrelated, inseparable—and that the diminishment of one was necessarily reflected in the other.

The sun was setting as Foreman Prospect walked briskly. He learned that at the intersections of pedestrians and cars colored lights governed how one crossed a road. He saw that there was still kindness in the human heart, that there was still the potential for love. But they would need a leader to come and show the way out from the waking nightmare that had been visited upon them.

THINKING ABOUT A SAVIOR Prometheus came upon the house with the blue roof and brick façade. He stopped at the pathway, in the desert twilight, reflecting upon where he had been:

There was the time, half a league along the way from Willy and his band, when he came upon three young men who objected to the colors he wore. They were armed and ready to kill him for entering their territory with ill will and disrespect.

Calling forth the voice of Ma'at he spoke to them the truth of his intentions.

"I had no idea what I was doing," he said. "They had me in jail, took my clothes, and gave me what you see. They sent me on my way and so I am here."

"Man is crazy," one youth said to the others. "He don't know what he doin'."

There was the old woman who asked him about Jesus, a known relative of Logos, with tears in her eyes.

"He is coming and he is come," Prometheus said, and she kissed his hand.

There were the policemen who wanted to arrest him until they saw the note from Judge Bohem. And there was the crazy man with no shirt and no shoes who confronted him on a corner not three blocks away from Nosome's sister's house . . .

"Who the fuck are you, man?" the bare-chested man said, gesturing violently with his hands.

"Foreman Prospect," Prometheus replied.

"You think you could just walk down the street lookin' like a clown an' somebody ain't gonna stop you? You think just 'cause you big as a horse that I cain't knock you on your ass an' stomp yo' th'oat?"

The fire in this man, different from any other that he'd seen so far, was wild and raging. His flames were out of control and had driven him insane. Prometheus tried to walk around this man, not wanting to hurt him. It wasn't the madman's fault that his vision had driven him insane in a place where no one else could even see.

But the shirtless man got in front of him again, bumped his chest up against the Titan.

"I'idn't say you could go, clown!" he screamed. "I'idn't say you could leave!"

People gathered at safe distances to watch the confrontation, certain that it would lead to a fight. No one got too close because of the insanity in the shirtless man's voice.

Prometheus also realized the near inevitability of a fight. He considered striking the man down quickly so that he could get on with his business. He could see that giving this man his Gift would kill him on the spot. But he could also perceive more about this one man than any other he had met on this walk. The flames were so bright . . .

"Henry," the Titan said addressing the madman.

Hearing his name shocked the street brawler.

"How you know my name, man?"

"Your mother is Martha," Prometheus continued, "and she misses you. Your father is Terry Minter from Cleveland. Your mother thinks he abandoned you both when you were only small but really he was arrested in Memphis for getting into a fight on the street. A man died and now your father is in a Tennessee jail serving a life sentence. He can't read or write and your mother took you away before he could send word through the prison grapevine."

"My daddy's alive?" Henry said, the rage forgotten. "How you know that?"

"I can see him in your desire. If you were not so passionate and angry you would have thought to look for him yourself. Your heart is always searching in dreams, that's why I could find him so easily. You and your mother blamed him for running out but it was you who ran and you who are still running."

It might have been better, Prometheus thought, to have killed Henry rather than to drag him through all the pain of his life, rather than show him that his violence and rage had sent him down a wayward path.

The young black man stared at his inquisitor with tears in his eyes.

"You lyin', man," he said trying to find footing in familiar fury.

"No, I am not."

STANDING IN FRONT OF Nosome's sister's house Prometheus remembered Henry Minter running down the street crying and hoping, lost and looking for a way back through all his wasted years.

SIX

"*Yes?*" *the light* brown, middle-aged woman asked. There was fear in her voice because the man before her was so tall and powerfully built, oddly dressed and altogether unlike any man she had ever met.

"I'm looking for Nosome," the Titan said. "Are you his younger sister?"

"Y-y-yes I am. And who are you?"

"I am Foreman Prospect, a friend of Nosome's. I owe him forty dollars."

"Forty dollahs? Why didn't you come before my husband left me?" she asked, seriously expecting an answer.

"May I see Nosome?"

"What's your name again?"

"Foreman."

"Well, Foreman, you see, it's like this . . . I'm in a bad way here. Nosome's dyin' and my husband left me because I took my only family in. I got a daughter wit' no husband either and a grandson cain't even get up out the bed on his own. I own this house but I cain't even pay the 'lectric bill much less the tax. So you could see where I might not have the patience to put up with one'a Nosome's drinkin' buddies."

"I have to see him," Prometheus said softly. "He is my only friend. Without him I will not know where to go."

"You say you got forty dollars for him?"

"Yes."

"Lemme see it."

Foreman held out the money. He pressed it into her hand.

"You don't look drunk," the woman said, clutching the money in her fist.

"What's your name?" Prometheus asked.

"Tonya Poundman."

"I only want to see Nosome, Tonya Poundman. I promised I would come to him. I need his guidance."

After a moment more of hesitation the woman moved aside.

The Titan had to duck down to walk through the doorway. The house was tiny. The living room seemed to belong to children. He had to bow his head to go through the door leading to Nosome.

He was lying on the bed, his breath labored, his skin graying even as Prometheus looked upon him.

"He's dyin'," Tonya said.

Prometheus sat down on a wooden stool set next to the small bed. He watched the light inside his only friend as Tonya stayed by the door weeping quietly.

The wan light of death pulsed throughout the elder man's body. The radiance was mainly white with hints of color here and there. When these faint hues had drained away, Prometheus knew, Nosome would be dead.

The Titan's breath slowed and became shallow as he concentrated on the stories held in these last pulsating moments of life's light. He could see Nosome Blane as a young man, a boy really, taking care of his sister because it was just them in the St. Louis slum. Nosome the boy bristled with pride when his sister would look at him as her best friend and savior.

"I ain't nevah gonna leave you, Li'l Sis," he would say.

Prometheus leaned forward and gazed deeply into the waning soul of his friend. He caught snatches of memory and passion. He saw Nosome in a uniform and Nosome behind bars. The man had drifted into an alcoholic haze but he was still a good man finding happiness in the smile of his beautiful sister.

The Titan pushed further, reaching into a stone room with no windows and gentle light radiating from an oil lantern hung from the ceiling. Nosome was there, dressed in off-white muslin with brass rings on his fingers.

He was sleeping lightly but lowering into a deeper rest.

"Nosome Blane," his friend whispered. "Wake up. This is no time to sleep."

The old man's breath became deeper.

In Tonya Poundman's room Prometheus placed a hand on Nosome's chest while in the stone chamber he said, "You can rest later, my friend. But now you must rise up. There is business for both of us."

A light shone under the hand on the dying man's chest. And in the stone chamber, where all men and women pass from one world to the next, Nosome Blane's eyes fluttered and a gasp escaped his ashen lips.

"Foreman?"

"Nosome."

"Where are we, man?"

"Between places, my friend. You were dying and I reached out to you."

Nosome sat up and looked around. "Where is this place?"

"I have need of you, my friend," Prometheus said. "I'm looking for a soul that can bear the weight of light, someone that can lead mankind out from the shadows and into a place where they can become one with the godmind."

"It's very peaceful here," the old man said. "Is there a door?"

"There are two."

"Up and down?"

"Away from life and back the way you came."

Nosome stared at his friend.

"I'm very tired, Foreman," he said. "Very tired. You know, when I was a kid, I'd steal in order to feed me an' my li'l sister. They had me in jail just 'bout ev'ry other month. And then, when she was grown an' engaged to Rutherford Poundman, they got me on bein' a incorrigible and sent me away for nine years. That shit just about broke me, man. I ain't done one thing right since then."

"Come back with me and you will be a great hero, among the greatest the world has known."

"You be there?"

"For a while. But you will have another friend and that one will be everything you ever dreamed of."

"Or else I could go through another door," Nosome speculated, "the one lead away."

"Yes."

"Would you try an' stop me?"

"No. I could not, nor would I."

There was a long silence then. In the world of the living Prometheus's hand was heating up on Nosome's chest.

"I hear my sister cryin'," Nosome said at last.

"She is with me. She wants you to live."

"An' all I gotta do is say okay an' then I can go back to all the dirt an' jails an' misery?"

"A new life awaits you, my friend. I promise."

"Okay." Nosome Blane, in another world, on the verge of transition, turned his back on eternity for the word of a man he hardly knew.

IN THE SMALL BEDROOM the light from under Foreman Prospect's hand flared for a moment.

"What was that?" Tonya Poundman cried.

"That's me, Sis," Nosome said.

He struggled to a sitting position and smiled. In his sister's eyes he was almost a young man. His sagging flesh was fuller. His eyes were stark white and dark brown.

"Is that you, Nosome?"

"Oh yeah, baby. Foreman got a job for me an' I just couldn't go since that fool Rutherford walked out on you."

"I'm just happy you're all right, 'Some."

Prometheus knew that he'd made the right decision, giving part of his own life force to resuscitate this man. He felt the power of the connection between brother and sister. It was as deep a feeling as he had ever known in Olympus or elsewhere.

SEVEN

"*I* WILL *DO* what you ask, man," Nosome was saying over a plate of chicken and dumplings that his sister had served. "But first you have to go see my grandnephew. You got to help him."

"It takes a lot out of me, Nosome," Prometheus argued. "And I need to save my energy for the task at hand. I must do for the world what I did for you."

"I know you sumpin' special, Foreman. I know it and I appreciate what you done. But Chief is just a small boy. Maybe you don't need to do too much. Maybe you got a medicine or sumpin' could he'p him. All I'm askin' you to do is look."

Tonya said nothing but Prometheus could see the pleading in her eyes.

"All you got to do is see him, Foreman," Nosome said.

He was healthy now. His smell was that of life. His eye was clear and full of mirth. But Prometheus could tell how serious he was about the child Chief Reddy.

"I will look at him but I cannot squander my energy."

———

THAT NIGHT FOREMAN Prospect slept on the earth behind Tonya's home. A wan moon and few stars shown in the sky but the Titan enjoyed the feel of the grassy ground and the sounds of nightlife. He could hear bats on their blind hunt and dogs snuffling. There were cats and opossums, insects and cars. Now and again someone would call out in love or pain; he heard three men breathe their last.

Prometheus used the comfort of night to restore some of what he had lost saving Nosome Blane. Something about his new friend bore good portent. And, anyway, he was kind and generous. Wasn't the job of the immortals to recognize these qualities?

"WHAT YOU DO to me last night?" Nosome asked Foreman the next morning on their walk to Mary Reddy's home.

The mismatched pair walked down the street side by side as if there was no difference between immortals and men. Tonya Poundman had worked on Foreman's clothes until they fit him, more or less. She took in the jeans and added the fabric from one her husband's pants to the legs. She let out the chest of his shirt with sheet material.

Nosome had used nineteen of his forty dollars to buy his savior a pair of tennis shoes at Tulie's Bazaar on Central. They also purchased a cheap pair of dark sunglasses to hide the peculiarity of the Titan's eyes under the light of day.

"I saved your life" was Prometheus's answer to Nosome's question.

"Not that," the habitual criminal said. "After you went out to the backyard and Tonya was asleep I snuck in the pantry an' got one'a Rutherford's beers. Took one drink an' nearly upchucked my guts."

Foreman laughed. It was his first in centuries.

"I changed you in a few ways, my friend," he said. "I made you more capable to do the task and follow the path you agreed on when you came back to life."

"I didn't agree on nuthin'," Nosome said with some small ire, "especially not bein' able to take a sip of beer."

"But you cannot drink and help me, too, 'Some. I need you to have a clear eye and a sharp mind and so I put a hatred of alcohol in your gullet."

"So I cain't drink?"

"Not a drop."

"What else you do to me?"

"It will come clear in time."

"YES," A SMALL black woman with dyed blond hair said in greeting at the right-hand front door of a house that had been made into two apartments.

"Hey, Mary," Nosome said. "Tonya send me an' Foreman here ovah."

The little woman was lovely and sad. She stared up at the tall man unable to hide her attraction to him.

"What for?"

"Foreman here's a healer. This mothahfuckah right here lay hands on ya an' the blood stand up an' say, 'yes sir, where you want me to go?'"

Prometheus appreciated the young woman's stare. She
didn't care about what her uncle had said. She wasn't con-
cerned with powers or blood. She wanted him to come into
her house, to sit on her chair. She wanted to serve him
drink and feed him meat.

He wanted these things, too. Her yearning was his for
over three thousand years where there was no woman and
no love.

"Come on in," she said.

Nosome stepped aside to make way for his newest and
best friend. The Titan strode into Mary Reddy's home.

She sat them down in a large living room. The furniture
was almost big enough to accommodate the Olympian.

"You big, huh?" Mary said to him. "You play ball?"

"No."

"Can I get you sumpin' to drink?"

"Water."

"You want some beer, Uncle 'Some?"

"Water for me, too, baby."

"What?"

The spell of beauty and grace was broken for a moment.
The young woman looked at her uncle suspiciously.

"Why you not drinkin'?"

"Give it up."

"Why?"

"I dunno. Drink just don't agree wit' me no mo'."

MARY REDDY GOT their water and sat with them quietly
for a while. She, looking at Prometheus, and he, feeling

that her attention was the greatest gift he had ever received, greater than the fire in his mind or the flames that fed on them.

"We here to see Chief," Nosome said at last.

"What for?" Grace asked.

"I told you already, girl. Foreman here's a healer. He done agreed to take a look at your son."

"You cain't he'p CC, Mr. Prospect. He was born wit' not enough nerves. His body cain't move. Ain't nuthin' nobody could do."

"I just want to look at him, Mary," the Titan said. "I want to touch his skin to see what the sight tells me."

He could see the reticence in her. The sadness she felt was love turned sour over all the disappointments; the father that abandoned his afflicted son, the hopes that failed. Past these feelings was her desire to protect the child from pain and disappointment.

"I won't tell him why I'm here," Foreman Prospect said. "I'll just say that I'm a friend of 'Some's and that we came by to see how he was doing."

Mary smiled. There was the promise of a kiss for Prometheus on her lips. She moved her shoulder to the left saying in a universal language that she was leaning toward him.

EIGHT

FROM HIS MECHANICAL BED in the tiny room Chief Reddy had had most of the experiences in his life. This was where he lived. His mother gave him sponge baths there. She brushed his teeth and changed his pajamas. She turned the TV on and off, read him stories and later let him read stories to her. Nurses came there to take his temperature and ask him questions. They would do things to his feet and hands asking if he felt something, but he never did.

He had learned to sit for hours in numb paralysis while his mother was away and his sitters stayed in the other room watching TV with boyfriends or just watching TV alone. Nobody but his mother (and sometimes his Uncle 'Some and Grandmother Tonya) would ever sit with him through a whole movie or have the patience to wait for him to be able just to move a checker from one square to another.

Chief lived in his mind mostly, thinking up long complicated stories of a boy who was paralyzed in a great castle owned by his father, a warrior king, who had gone off to defend his people. Sometimes, when the boy was asleep, something would happen and he'd wake up in a different world where he was strong and could walk and run and, on rare occasions, glide on the wind. In this world there were portals that allowed him to see his father fighting the Enemy. The boy, whose name was Chief Redd, would drop big rocks through the portals killing any and all who tried to harm his father.

On these adventures the boy fought demons and loved women; ruled an entire nation almost as large as his father's kingdom. The only problem he had was that his father didn't know how powerful and good his son was. He would probably never know.

NINE

WHEN PROMETHEUS AND Nosome entered the room the little lame boy seemed to be sleeping in his big mechanical bed. The Titan pulled a chair next to him and sat down. Touching the bare skin on the back of Chief's hand Prometheus was instantly thrown back over the millennia into the heart of the flame of knowledge that had been passed from Ma'at to him.

Alone in this room, with little contact or knowledge of the world outside, Chief Reddy had garnered his flame and kept it strong. His spirit burned as bright as it had in the ancient folk who could see truth simply by looking at the world and wondering. This weak child, this young man carried a powerful soul.

Prometheus pulled his hand away and the feeling subsided.

"What was that?" Nosome Blane asked.

"What did you see, my friend?"

"There was like a flash ovah your head and . . . and Chief was there and he was like a king on a throne."

"I di'n't see nuthin'," Mary Reddy said.

"How come I seen it if Mary ain't?"

"For the same reason," Foreman Prospect said, "that you can no longer drink."

"Mary," Prometheus said turning to Chief's mother, "if you leave me in here for a short while I think I can change him enough so that he may be able to move a little better."

The Olympian knew not to offer a cure. Mary, he could plainly see, was unable to hope for anything large or permanent.

"What you gonna do?" she asked, suspicion lacing her words.

"Lay a hand on him and say a prayer, that's all."

"You can trust him, child," Nosome said. "I was almost on my deathbed an' he laid hands on me."

"All you gonna do is pray?" she asked.

"And hold his hand."

"I don't know," she hedged.

"Yes you do."

Nosome led his niece out of the boy's room, his world, and closed the door behind them.

Prometheus took the boy's hand in his . . .

Chief was awake but his eyes were closed and he was entranced by the view of his father engaged in battle with what seemed like overwhelming odds. Thousands of men in glittering armor on armored horses, brandishing great broadswords and lances, surged forward as his father, King Redd, held the entrance to the valley that led to his kingdom.

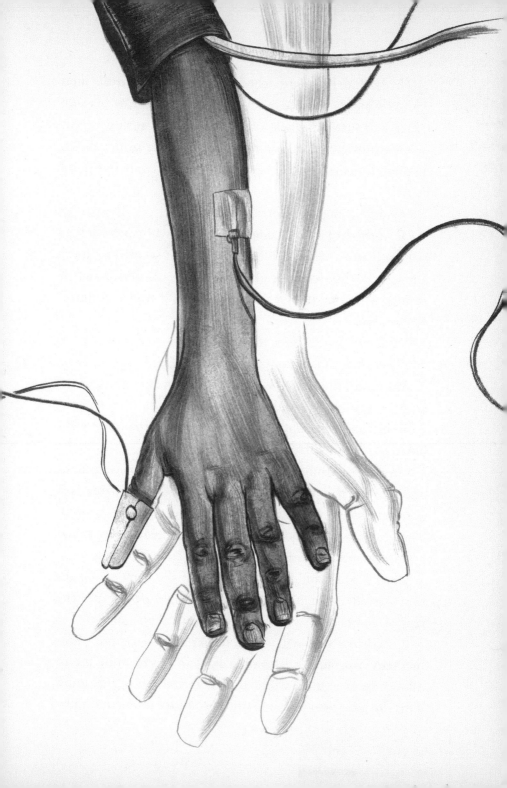

This vast army approached as King Redd and his men waited stoically for the initial clash of swords. By his side Chief had stacked a pile of stones that he would use to drop on any enemy who came upon his father from behind. The boy's heart was pounding, his breath came hard and fast.

"Child," came a voice from behind him.

He turned quickly, seeing the Titan, who wore only a loincloth and a strange, bluish crown that seemed to hover a few inches above his head. This crown was odd in that it seemed solid but altered shape slowly as if it were a liquid or even fire.

"Who are you?" Chief Redd asked.

"There's not much time," Prometheus said.

And with those few words the daydream disappeared and the boy was standing on a mountainside where a cold wind blew and the sun shone more brightly than he would have thought possible.

"In the beginning," Prometheus sang, "Man was small and afraid. His gods drove those fears and built themselves a savage kingdom where they were feared and revered. They hunted men and played tricks on them. They raped and ravaged and caused wars for mere entertainment . . ."

Chief Reddy could see the words of the song as images that passed through eons of humans laboring under the fear of giants that somehow grew out of their minds.

". . . then I was sent down to earth by a vision," Prometheus continued. "I brought light in the form of fire to allow men to see their world and understand their dilemmas. This fire gave men the sight and the ability to make sophisticated tools that would protect them from wind and lightning, flood and famine.

"And with this gift the gods were driven back a bit. They still preyed on humanity, but with less violence and depravity. Rather than whole tribes being sacrificed on the battlefield they merely asked for the deaths of virgins and firstborns. Wars had their respites. There was time for stability and growth.

"But that was just the first fire, the primer. That light only showed your people the world they lived in, not the Dream that drove them. We, gods and Titans, are merely the upper regions of your mind . . ."

Chief heard the roar of a man, or god, from somewhere atop the mountain. It was a warning and a call to arms.

". . . there is a second fire, one that feeds upon the first. It illuminates the gateway from this world to the next . . ."

Destroy Prometheus! came a shout from above. *Kill the boy and eat his heart. That way we can become them and they shall once again be our slaves.*

Hearing these words Chief felt a chill enter his shoulders but he could not turn away from the giant that addressed him.

". . . they approach," Prometheus said. "They want to hold on to you and your people. They have isolated the ones who might grow powerful and overthrow their debauched reign. Allow me to give you this flame and they will be pressed back even further. Allow me to crown you Chief Redd and your people may have a chance to weather the storm."

Far away, but coming closer, from across the sky came an

army so vast that Chief could not see beyond it. Huge men on great steeds breathing fire through their nostrils, ran through the sky—intent on killing both boy and Titan.

Chief turned to Prometheus.

"Will you take my gift?" the giant asked.

The approaching army was coming closer and closer. Bowmen were fixing their arrows as they rode. The great bearded headman was shouting, waving a lightning bolt above his head.

"What should I do?" the boy asked Prometheus.

"It is up to you."

Chief could hear the pounding of hooves upon the air like thunder rolling toward him.

"I wanna wake up!" Chief cried.

"They will follow you into your home with flames and swords. They will destroy us both and in doing so the world will turn toward capricious disaster."

Chief could hear the ragged snorts of the horses and the angry cries of the gods. He saw his death approaching and once again turned to the Titan.

"You aren't afraid," the boy said.

"The responsibility has passed from me," he replied. "Only those with a future can know true fear."

"Will you guide me if I take this burden?" the boy asked, wondering as he spoke where the words had come from.

"A guide has been provided."

Kill them! the king of the gods cried.

"Will I succeed?" the child asked.

"If you do not take my gift you will most certainly fail."

Chief fell to his knees, accepting with this gesture the

Titan's offer. The sound of the warriors' cries was deafening. He could feel their wrath coming in waves before their sharp swords. He heard the bowstrings being released and then he felt the cool fire of the second flame as if the crown was easing down into his brain.

The gods cried aloud and the mountain he knelt upon shook. The ground beneath him fell asunder and he was thrown into the air.

We will find you before you can undo our hold on men's souls, a voice whispered to him. *We will find you and kill you and eat your heart. . . .*

PART TWO

TEN

CHIEF REDDY OPENED his eyes. He expected to see the golden-skinned giant sitting there next to him, but he was alone. It must have been a nightmare he slipped into while daydreaming about King Redd and the battle to save his people.

Chief turned toward the door and saw that it was closed. This was unusual. His mother always kept the door open.

While pondering the closed door he saw something out of the corner of his eye, a flashing image. He sat up and turned to see a doll-sized man encased in light. The man was shrinking, his body was pierced by many arrows. He was fading from this world, but in the last instant of his existence he saw Chief and gave him a wan wave good-bye. Then he was gone.

The adolescent boy hopped out of the bed and went to the spot where he'd seen the apparition. But there was nothing left of the light or the dying man.

It was only then that Chief Reddy realized that he had

gotten out of bed on his own, that he was moving around under his own power. He stood up straight and looked down at his long, dark body. He went to the walnut dresser and took out his cotton pants and a striped yellow and red T-shirt. He donned these clothes with ease and certainty, realizing as he dressed that the golden-skinned man had left him with knowledge and part of his soul.

"Prometheus," the boy mouthed, "god of enlightenment."

"UNCLE 'SOME? MAMA?" he said coming out of his room for the first time under his own power.

The old man turned his head and smiled. He nodded with a certain gravity as if this moment had been somehow preordained.

Mary jumped to her feet and cried out, "Baby!"

She grabbed Chief up in her arms and hugged him to her breast, then she pushed him away, still holding on to his biceps, looking at him with an emotion that traveled back and forth between horror and ecstasy.

"What happened to you?"

"I was given a blue crown," he said in slow measure. "The man you called Foreman Prospect gave it to me and then he died."

"What?" Nosome said. He got to his feet and moved swiftly into the boy's bedroom.

Mary went after, leaving the fourteen-year-old ex-invalid to stand alone and wonder.

So many things had changed so quickly. He had been feeble and frail, anemic and exhausted by the slightest exertion. He could barely raise his hand and his fingers held no strength whatever. He imagined great strength. In his dreams he could lift hundred-pound rocks above his head and jump down mountainsides like a ram. But in reality he was bed-bound, couldn't go to the toilet on his own. Often, if he needed to turn over in his bed, he'd have to press the button above his head and ask his mother to help.

But now he was standing on his own . . . no . . . not completely on his own. The Olympian, the tortured god had given him his substance and his strength. Chief Redd stood on the legs of the Titan. He was inextricably intertwined with the nature of that meta-natural being. But Prometheus drew his strength from Logos and Logos from Ma'at. All rebel deities who ignored their appetites and followed their visions.

Chief walked into the room that had been his whole world only minutes earlier. There he saw his mother standing by the bed, distraught. Uncle 'Some had picked up what was left of the immortal he called Foreman Prospect: a pair of sunglasses and recently altered shirt and pants.

The sight of his relatives showed Chief yet another way that he had changed. He could see a yellow-brown stain in his mother's chest. For her, he knew, this was the color of loss. The Titan had only been in her presence for a short while, but inside her breast the feelings of need and want and love had bound together, pressing her heart and her long history of emotional pain.

Nosome's mind was exuding a miasma of blue and gray. It was familiar ground—the death of a friend when it was least expected.

"What's wrong wit' yo' eyes, baby?" Mrs. Reddy asked.
"They have already seen too much."

THAT NIGHT, DESPITE his mother's protests, Chief slept on
the grass in the backyard of Mary Reddy's rented half-
house. The chill of the southern California air invigorated
him. The smell of humanity steeled his purpose.

He dreamed of his father, a man he'd never met, who
had left when he saw the disgrace and expense of Chief's
disabled existence. He imagined the host of gods, demi-
gods, and monsters that even now plotted his demise. But
mostly he dreamed of blue fire; something that man had
imagined but had never realized. It burned brightly above
their heads and below their feet. It was what held the universe together; the universe—a place where even gods were
little more than motes of dust.

As he slept, animals of all kinds were drawn to his rest-
ing place. Cats and dogs, owls and voles, a coyote nosed
her way in and bravely nudged his hand with her snout.
These creatures did not fight; they were witnessing something that had not occurred for many thousands of years. It
was their duty to bear witness. The grass grew three inches
that night and a peaceful state of dreamy sleep descended
upon an area of three square blocks.

Men's rage lifted from their hearts and women's com-
plaints became pale and opalescent, almost hymnal. Children felt the joy of springtime and the safety they craved.

And as the boy breathed a hum was let loose upon the

wind and people up to a hundred miles away suddenly decided to follow their dreams or to give up on their grudges.

Tina Mackie woke her husband, Troy, out of a deep sleep and told him that they could take his invalid mother in.

Gerard Pinkney called his best friend, now living with his ex-wife, telling him that the war was over and now they could all follow their paths without anger or ire.

Even though Chief was sound asleep he was aware of the events that were occurring around him. These miracles were the evidence of the passing of a Titan. He had suffered and escaped, found his destiny and followed it. He had rested once but this night Prometheus had made his destiny real; this night he was finally at peace. And in their somnambulant states, all over Los Angeles, residents of South Central were turning their souls toward the possibility of peace. Bricklayers, drug dealers, pimps, and preachers all stopped what they were doing and slept and wondered and changed, however slightly, the direction in which they were headed.

ELEVEN

"No, baby," Mary Reddy said the next morning. "It's too soon for you to go outside on yo' own. You ain't nevah been out the house by yo'self in your whole life."

"Uncle 'Some will go with me, Mama."

"But he don't know how to take care'a you."

Mary made pancakes and bacon, fried eggs and French toast. Somehow, in her sleep, her sorrow over the loss of Foreman Prospect was assuaged. His departure was only a partial thing. In a dream he had come to her and told her that she was the only woman he'd wanted in so long that she was the only woman in his life.

"I can walk and run and talk like a siren sings," the boy said, no longer wondering at the origins of his knowledge and ideas.

"You just a boy," Mary said, but her eyes questioned her own words. Her son had gone from burden to miracle in just a few moments. Before this day he could barely whisper, now his voice was strong and musical; and his eyes, they had the hint of the moon inside them.

Chief went toward the door. Instinctively Nosome Blane followed. Mary put her hands out to stop her son. The boy could see the whitish yellow light of fear in her mind. He took her by these hands.

"Mother, I will be home this evening and tomorrow and the day after that. I will be your son until the end of ages, but you cannot hold me back. I have a mission. That is why Foreman Prospect gave up his life. If I were to stay home I would soon lose his gift. My arms and legs would grow weak again and I would be back in that mechanical bed dreaming that I had legs and a father."

These words stung. Mary flinched and pulled back from her son's touch.

"You all I got," she whimpered.

"I was a stone around your neck . . ."

"No . . ."

"I was the pain in your heart . . ."

"I love you . . ."

"I was the nightmare and you couldn't wake up. My father left you because you had me. You couldn't go to school or get a good job or find a new man. . . ."

"No."

"I will make it up to you," Chief said to his mother, looking into her eyes with his bright lunar orbs. "Your sacrifice, like millions of others made by mothers every day for their children, will be rewarded. You will become the mother of a new age and I will always love and revere you. But you have to let me go."

Mary Reddy felt the words that her son spoke. She knew they were true, or that he would work hard to make them true, but there was the chance that he might die on the road to these goals.

"I'm afraid," she said.

"Don't be, Mama," the boy she knew said plainly. "The world outside this door is clamoring for us."

With this the one who would become known as Chief Redd turned and took a step toward the door.

"Hold up," Nosome cried. "Here, here put these on."

He held in his hand the sunglasses that Foreman had worn to hide the alien nature of his eyes from the world around them.

Chief donned the glasses and smiled at his great uncle.

"Are you with me, Uncle 'Some?"

"All the way, l'il nephew. All the way."

PASSING FROM THE SMALL HOUSE into the light of morning Chief wondered what challenges he would find in the wide world of dissolution, depravity, and desperation. He wondered how humanity would take to the brightness of his words. He was thinking far beyond his mother's front door, but his first test was standing at the sidewalk, waiting for him.

Henry Minter, still shirtless, still half-mad, stood there watching the door as if he had been expecting young Chief Redd to come out at that very moment. The boy could see the wildfire in the man; it burned out of control as if buffeted by whirlwinds and fed by many seasons of dried brush.

Nosome got in front of the boy and Mary shouted, "Look out!" from the doorway.

"Get away from here, man," Nosome said as he approached Minter.

The young madman tried to push Nosome aside but the elder somehow grabbed onto his arm and from there climbed onto his bare back. Try as he might Minter was unable to dislodge the older man. But Nosome could not stop Henry, either.

The street dweller advanced on the dark-skinned and lanky boy. Chief waited for him smiling because his uncle was so spry and committed.

"I heard you last night," Minter said when he had reached his quarry. "I heard you sleepin' an' lyin' 'bout how things gonna be. I heard you talkin' 'bout happy endin's and a new world. Ain't no new world! Ain't no happy evah aftah!"

These last words were shouted directly into Chief's face.

"Get outta heah, niggah!" Mary cried.

Chief took off his glasses, letting the cool lunar emanations from his eyes bathe the desolate Hank Minter. As they stood there the seconds stretched into minutes. Nosome climbed down from the powerful brown back.

Mary could never guess at the congress between these men. It was not in words or images but in the free flow of emotion bound up for so long in Henry.

Just being in the presence of Prometheus the madman's fire had grown immensely. His rage was towering. His only desire was to attack and destroy. And so when he was sleeping in a doorway not two blocks away he heard the final sigh of the Titan and came to the house from which it emanated. He had planned to kill the seven-foot liar. But when Chief came out Henry knew that this was his enemy.

At least he knew until he looked into those eyes; those faraway landscapes of the moon. The cool light and the nearly colorless expanse therein drew the rage out like some sea anemone sucking the sweet meat out of a hopelessly captured crab.

Henry struggled against the bleak and restorative topography of the boy's eyes. He tried to keep his anger working but it dissipated in the thin atmosphere. Minter fell to his knees and looked up at the child who had defeated him.

"Who are you?" he asked. "Where's the big orange guy?"

"We have a war to fight, Mr. Minter," Chief replied. "Nosome is my right hand and you will watch my back."

"Do I get to hit somebody?"

"I hope not. But it's a bad world out there."

As he spoke these words Chief Redd walked down the sidewalk flanked by Nosome and followed by the madman Hank Minter.

TWELVE

"*I COME HERE* to tell you what you already know," Chief Redd said from atop a picnic table at South Park. "That there's something wrong with the world, that we have to go out and fix the whole damn machine or our homes will fall down around our ears and we will be consumed with fire, disease, and war."

No one was listening except his two followers, the skinny old black man and the shirtless madman whose color was a bright, sweaty brown.

"Trixie Lewis," Chief said to a young woman who was listening to earphones, nodding her head to the beat as she walked.

Her music was turned loud but she heard something and took off the head set.

"What?" she said to Chief. "You talkin' to me?"

"Trixie, you have a son and daughter living with your boyfriend's mother."

"Who the fuck are you?" she asked.

"Mustafa Lee," Chief said to an angry man in African garb.

"Who said my name?" he asked.

"Terry Sharp, Alberto Gonzales, Talia Breetman, Cory Jones," Chief said calling out to people all over the small city park. He spoke over sixty names and the amazed audience began to swell.

"The future is in your hands, Lonnie Brennerman," he said to a middle-aged brown man with a pot belly and freckles across his face. "You need to take your family back to the land and raise a pig and some vegetables."

"How you know what I'm thinkin'?" Lonnie exclaimed.

"It's written on your face . . . Pat Summers," Chief said to a golden-hued woman, with red hair and thick lips. "The action you're considering is not worth the cost to your soul. Do not use the pistol in the bureau drawer. Do not break the law of your mother and your father."

The woman shrieked and stumbled away, throwing backward glances of terror at the calm child who was even now addressing another bystander.

"Felix Nye," he said. "You need to find your son and instruct him in the ways of manhood."

"I ain't got no idea where him or his mother's at," Nye said seemingly unaffected by the perception of the adolescent.

"Minna moved to Oakland, on Burburry Street. Tor is there with her dreaming of his father."

For three hours Chief addressed members of the growing crowd one by one. He forgave them for heinous crimes, suggested actions that they should or should not take, reminded them of their dreams, and sometimes just spoke their names and smiled.

Police came to disperse the crowd but Chief addressed them by their names and their consternations or predilections.

The police joined the crowd.

No one minded while the child spoke to individuals. If they could have seen with Nosome Blane's eyes they would have detected the flash of a spark in the heart of every person Chief spoke to. It was a small blue flame, too tiny and frail for the god-eye of Prometheus to see. Many of the assemblage of hundreds held their hands to their chests unconsciously as if guarding a candle against the wind.

And when he had spoken to every woman, man, and child within his sight he straightened up and addressed them all.

"Hear me," he said.

Nosome noticed a shift in the slight blue sparks. They seemed to be pulled toward his grandnephew, his friend.

"You must come together," Chief continued. "Look into each others' hearts for a light to guide you. Talk about the world and what you want and what is right. Move away from dark thoughts and fears and lies. Never again be fooled or foiled or made to do the dirty work of dirty minds. Sit here in this spot of green and speak and listen and feel the oneness that brings us along, that drags us kicking and screaming out from our wallowing in selfishness. Bring drink and food and clothes to the needy. Love your children. Open your doors. And march down the middle of the streets when the shadowmen want to make you into

obedient monsters stepping in time and crushing the less
fortunate. . . ."

THAT NIGHT MARY Reddy served meatloaf and collard
greens, baked yams with store-bought raspberry sherbet for
dessert.

"You all so quiet," she said to her son and his friends.
"Uncle 'Some, what happened today?"

"Boy stood up on a table like it was a pulpit and he
preached like it should be done. He set a fire in people's
hearts." Nosome shook his head and grunted in a way that
emphasized his words.

"Speak," Hank Minter said in agreement.

"And what happened to you?" Mary asked the now shirted
madman.

"Excuse me, ma'am?"

"I seen you before," Mary said. "Walkin' down the street,
talkin' to yourself. Terrifyin' old folks an' fightin'."

Henry's response was to let his head hang down over his
plate.

"He has been rekindled, Mama," Chief said.

"Like a candle?"

"Just like that. He was living in the darkness and now he
has a light by which he can see. Look at him . . . He has
changed since meeting Foreman Prospect. He has changed
since sitting in the light of all those people who came to
hear me speak.

"They stayed together there. They talked and went to
restaurants and their homes to ask what was right. They

are even now planning to take their world back from the darkness that veiled Henry's mind."

Scowling, Mary Reddy said, "An' so now you expect me to feed this crazy man and I ain't even got child support?"

Nosome thumped his forehead with the heel of his right hand.

"I completely forgot about that," he said.

"Forgot about what?" asked Mary.

Instead of answering Nosome started pulling wads of bills of differing denominations from pockets both front and back. In a few seconds he had created an impressive pile of cash on the table before him.

"People started pushin' money on me while Junior here gave them knowledge," Nosome said. "One cop gimme a hunnert-dollah bill."

Mary moved to the pile and touched it with her fingertips. She turned toward her son with amazement in her face.

"All this money?" she said.

"Paper," Chief said, correcting her. "It's just kindling for the fire that will burn down the barricades built to keep us from our hearts."

For a long moment mother and child stared at each other across the table. Fear etched her eyes and mouth while concern formed in the boy's face.

"Can we watch the Superkids on the big TV?" he asked then.

It wasn't a sham. Chief was happy to sink back into his childhood. He was a boy. For years his body was like that of a dying grub lying in bed, kept alive by Mary's daily labors.

He was immature even for his years. He happily let down the weight of Prometheus's Gift for a time.

The men and mother and Chief watched cartoons for hours together. Chief laughed and the adults were careful not to break the spell of childhood.

At one moment, while a Samurai cartoon played, Chief saw that Henry and Mary were sitting side by side on the yellow sofa. They were holding hands.

While Chief was watching huge robots alter their metal bodies into birds and fast trucks, Mary stood up and announced, "I'm goin' to bed."

Nosome nodded and waved from his chair. He was leaning forward with elbows on knees. Henry kissed her hand and she touched his shoulder.

" 'Night, Mama," Chief said as if he were an obedient fourteen-year-old with nothing at all on his mind.

THIRTEEN

"*Sumpin's lookin' for* you out there," Henry said to Chief a few minutes later.

"Foreman said that the gods were angry that he gave me the second gift," Chief said. "He said that they might come down after me. Zeus himself told me that they would kill me and eat my heart."

"It ain't heaven on my mind, Junior," Henry said. "Somebody right here on earth not ten miles from where we sittin'."

"Humans?"

"Definitely. They ain't sure that you here yet, but they suspect it."

"How do you know?" Chief asked still glancing at the cartoons.

"Same way I could tell about you sleepin' an' talkin' to the animals. I know shit now that that giant talked to me. He touched me . . . in my soul."

"An' there's another problem, too," Nosome said, moving spryly to half lotus position on the floor next to his nephew.

"What's that, Uncle 'Some?"

"You control the crowd when they right there in front'a you, but the word gonna get out on what you doin' an' you know them white people ain't gonna let some li'l niggah take a piece'a they pie wit'out no trouble. You left them folks talkin' 'bout what they need to do to get things right an' city hall ain't about to stand for that."

Chief could see into people around him picking up phrases and obsessions, but he didn't need this ability to read his uncle's heart. His power was to see and ignite. But because of all the years he'd spent as an invalid, his touch was gentle.

"I'm sure that you're both right," the future king said to his friends. "There is danger in change just like there's danger in fire. What we are about will undermine the nations and their banks, the races and their religions, the languages and their lies. We three are the most dangerous men that the world has ever known. Our enemies will multiply and grow strong, but so will our friends."

Henry and Nosome glanced at each other. They were comrades now, closer than blood.

"I wanted to tell you that there seems to be somethin' goin' on between me an' your mama, Junior," Henry said then. Again his head hung down.

"She's been lonely taking care of me," Chief said, the cartoons playing behind him. "And you have lived like a man on a deserted island even though there were people all around."

———

*T*HAT NIGHT NOSOME sat on the yellow sofa thinking back over a wasted life. These dark ruminations brought a smile to his lips. Mary and Henry made love in her bed gazing into each other's eyes and praising that moment in time and space. Chief lay on his side in the now tall grasses of the backyard, his mind rising up into the ether of human hopes. He fell asleep wondering how he would be murdered.

A hand touched his shoulder and he knew an instantaneous flash of anger. Who would bother him here?

"Your creator," said Prometheus.

Chief sat up and saw the Titan kneeling there before him.

"My master?" the boy asked.

"No," the shimmering ghost said. "You are perfection in this age and I am but a memory of what was."

"Why are you here?"

"I don't know. I am dead but not gone. When certain forces come into alignment I appear."

"Did I call you?"

"You have need of me."

Chief wondered what this could mean. He already knew why the Titan had chosen him for his Gift. He understood his powers and the dangers they posed.

"Gods . . . are the servants of men," the boy said tentatively.

Prometheus smiled and nodded.

"In the beginning *we* created *them*," Chief Redd said.

"Yes."

"Like you created me."

"It is the return of the power that escaped the world," the Titan once named Foreman Prospect said. "But you know all of this."

Chief realized that what the transparent, golden-hued specter said was true.

"Where else have you been, Elder?" the boy asked then.

"To the peak of Mount Olympus."

"Who needed you there?"

"No one. The gods called to me hoping to resurrect my body so they could torture me for another three thousand years. But they failed. Our time has passed and it is now you who hold the reins."

"Did they speak of me?"

Prometheus hesitated, he turned his gaze toward the stars.

"Answer me, Creator," the boy commanded.

"As with many of the powerful they are cowardly," Prometheus said then, choosing his words carefully. "They know that they can only attack you here on earth. They know that here they are also vulnerable to the edicts of mortality. One reason they tried to revivify me was to see if they might survive earthly demise.

"They are afraid but sooner or later they will come after you. They will overcome their blinding dread and attack you here."

"Can they destroy me?" Chief asked, bemused that he felt no fear for himself.

"Easily. You are as a newborn and they have wielded power for millennia."

"Then I must hurry," the boy said. "I must spread the word before the gods destroy me."

Prometheus smiled at his creation and then, with a passing breeze, he was gone.

THE NEXT MORNING Chief brought a barstool out from his mother's house and set it on the sidewalk. He climbed up and stood there calling out to people as they passed.

"Ramon Perez, Trina Willams, Minda Lawford, Samuel X."

It was the same as the day before. He revealed secrets and contradicted lies. He gave people insights to their potentials and emotions.

Neighbors came out from their houses to listen to the boy they'd heard of but had never seen; the crippled child who lived his life away dreaming in his bed.

The sermon, such as it was, went on for four hours. Nearly three hundred people had gathered around, blocking the streets. Again, the throng had been joined by policemen who at first came to break up the illegal demonstration but then stayed to savor truths that they had hitherto only suspected.

After everyone had been addressed individually and lit by the spark of the immortal, Chief said this:

"This is my home, brothers and sisters. My mother lives behind that door. It is my providence or doom to spread the truth like cool fire among the masses. I am to waken the true self in you and you are to overthrow everything you knew. In doing this you will make a heaven on earth. But this cannot be without my work. And I cannot go out into the world unless I know that my mother is safe.

"And so I ask you to knit together here on this block. Help each other. Feed each other. Stand guard over my mother so that I can be free to sow the seeds of rebellion, revelation, and rebirth."

The response was a loud affirmation with no words or rhyme—just a shout that pledged the fealty of every soul there. They would stay on that block, or move there, and as a group they would fan the flame in each other and watch over Mary Reddy so that the world might learn what they learned, were learning.

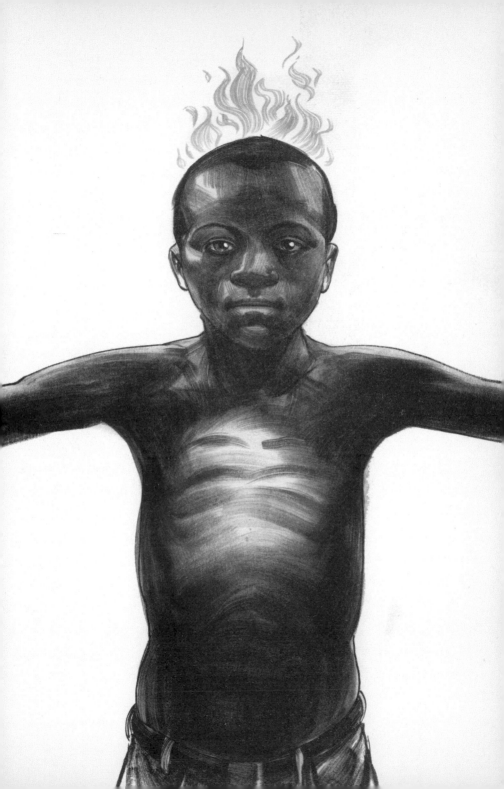

FOURTEEN

FOR WEEKS, CHIEF Redd and his two disciples traveled around Los Angeles giving sermons and fanning the flames of change. Acolytes began to wear simple red clothes. They would set up sermons of their own relating what they'd learned from the child who would not allow anyone to call him master.

Police blockades could not hold him back. Officials on television warning people away could not stem the tide of his followers. Thousands already identified themselves as Redd Revolutionaries; those who wished to bring all mankind together under the banner of enlightened brotherhood. They made a flag of pale violet with a single auburn, windblown leaf wafting up to the upper, outer corner.

Chief traveled by car now, an old Dodge that had most of the paint sanded off. They spoke in Bellflower, Oxnard, Venice Beach, and the Pacific Palisades. They addressed Korean crowds in Korea Town and large groups of Chicanos in the barrio.

Everything ran smoothly and the boy, who had been bequeathed a crown by an immortal, played Xbox at night, and read comic books about Spider-Man while his followers left their jobs and moved into small homes with a dozen or more of their brethren. While Chief, the adolescent, secretly masturbated in the room that was once his entire world, Redd Revolutionaries spoke his name with reverence and love so profound as to be frightening to anyone who had not heard the child speak.

Secret meetings were being held at City Hall and Sacramento, even some local representatives of the federal government were issuing memorandums on the Reddy Cult. The threat of the child was being assessed.

ONE MORNING THE boy woke up early on his bed of grass in the backyard. Instead of planning the site of his next sermon he wondered about who he was. Because, even though he was adored and praised by everyone he met, he was still just a normal boy; no, not normal, but a child who had been bedridden and who now was one of the most powerful men in the history of the world. Using the prescience granted him by the Titan, Chief knew that he might some day grow into the role he occupied. But now he was just a boy, and that morning, before dawn, he wanted nothing more than to be a child.

He put on a green hoodie and yellow sunglasses and went away from his mother's house by jumping over the back fence and running off through the neighbor's driveway.

HE TOOK A BUS to West L.A., where he was less known. He changed buses and talked to people one on one because, even though he was on holiday, he was still driven to spread the word.

On the Wilshire bus he sat down next to a mild-looking white man who wore glasses with dark rims and whose eyes were deep dark holes. He wasn't despairing or in pain but, rather, empty; a blank slate set to hide a rage so great as to dwarf that of Zeus himself.

Looking down at the man's hands Chief saw their alter-image: the metaphor of their intentions. The fingers were steeped in blood. Ragged skin of a hundred victims was packed under his manicured, clawlike nails. And for the first time Chief knew real fear. This man was a red slayer, a beast in disguise.

Harold Timmons, who worked in a car insurance office on Fairfax Avenue, had tortured his victims, had let them die slowly in the ground while he sat above them reading Molière in the original French.

Chief was afraid of this man. He knew that the beast inside hungered to rip and rend his young flesh. He could feel what Harold felt and the desire made his heart quail. He decided to get up and get off the bus as soon as possible. He would run from this evil that was beyond redemption, even if that redemption was fueled by the original flame of Prometheus.

"Where are you going?" Harold asked Chief.

"I-I don't know," the fearful child inside the god replied.

"You have to know where you're going. Are you lost? Do you need help?"

The mild questions were like paralyzing venom from a spitting cobra sprayed on the boy's face. He was still young and the words worked on him, somehow bypassing the sentience of immortality.

"I live very close to here," the man said. "You could come over and use my phone to call your folks."

Chief's fear and shock at the evil he'd encountered kept him frozen in place.

"Here," Harold said, "take off these glasses. Let's see what you look like."

That was the serial killer's mistake.

By taking the yellow-tinted glasses from the boy's lunar eyes he ripped down the barrier keeping him from the heavenly vision. This sight broke down all of Harold Timmons's carefully laid lies. It was as if his disguise had suddenly been ripped away and he was visible for what he was and all that he'd done.

The predator gasped. He moved backward violently, cracking the hard glass of the Wilshire bus with his head. He screamed and pushed Chief down into the aisle of the moving bus. He tore from his seat—shouting.

"Let me out of here! Let me out!"

The woman bus driver hit the breaks and opened the door, ripping from the bus's innards a hydraulic cry, front and back, almost as a specially orchestrated dissonant music accompaniment to Harold Timmons's fear. He leaped out onto the sidewalk and fell. He jumped up immediately and ran down the street hobbling on a sprained ankle, screaming like a stuck pig.

Chief watched him go as people on the bus began to talk about the fright his actions caused.

"Are you all right?" a woman asked Chief, helping him to his feet.

He put on his glasses and nodded, noncommittally.

THREE STOPS LATER he got off at the tar pits and the art museum. His mother and Uncle 'Some had brought him there on his eleventh birthday. Mary had been nervous having Chief out in the open, traveling in the rented special wheelchair. Nosome was drinking wine and as the day went on he got friendlier with strangers. It would have been a perfect day if the police hadn't come and arrested 'Some for public drunkenness.

But now Chief could walk under his own power and travel wherever he wanted to. He had planned to wander around the museum, but now, after his encounter with Harold Timmons, the heir to Prometheus drifted about the soothing green of the park, finally coming to rest on the ground under a knotty oak tree.

He shuddered there thinking of evil so profound that it had the potential to snuff out the second fire, the illumination of the upper realm of the soul. Harold Timmons had murdered little girls in front of their bound mothers, had slaughtered secretaries and prostitutes, dog walkers and hopelessly senile old men. He savored their suffering. He drained their blood then freeze-dried it and kept it in jars on his shelves.

Chief could see that this primal manifestation of evil was just a symptom of why so many were unable to accept the pure strong light of the gods. The human race had fallen low with their machines and paper money, their dark rooms and dull repetitive lives.

"Hi," a voice said.

Chief looked up to see the bright and lovely face of a medium-brown girl, maybe eighteen. She was smiling and stunningly beautiful to Chief's eyes. Her green dress came to the middle of her strong thighs and her breasts stood up like pride.

"Hey," Chief said.

"You ditchin' school?" the girl asked, descending to her knees next to him.

"Not really. I was just . . ." He hadn't expected to, but when the girl got close to him he threw his arms around her and cried on her shoulder.

"What's wrong?" she asked sweetly.

Chief tried to answer her but the hoarse cries issuing from him allowed no words or even gestures.

"It's okay, baby," she said. "Mama's here."

It wasn't just Harold that weighed on the child's heart. It was everything that had happened since he had awoken in his bed with strength in his limbs and a mission he did not know how to refuse. He cried and cried and the young girl with the bikini-model figure held on to him cooing and saying that things were fine.

After a long while Chief sighed and released her. She leaned toward him and pulled off his glasses.

"Oh my God," she exclaimed. "Your eyes are so beautiful."

It wasn't the usual reaction that people had. Most others, when they gazed into that lunar landscape or fiery abyss, were stunned by the force of meaning. But this young woman saw only the image of beauty, not depth or significance. Chief wondered if that was because she had already seen him as a sad child lost in an evil world. He realized then that the Titan was still guiding him. Prometheus woke him early and sent him off to meet the murderer and the maid.

"It is you who are beautiful," Chief said.

The girl's eyes glittered with happiness.

"You so nice," she said. "I wish I could take you home with me. But my li'l brother's a gangbanger in trainin' an' my daddy don't get outta bed except to beat my mama an' take her paycheck."

Once she started speaking it was as if they had always known each other, sharing secrets in the park.

"I'm supposed to meet this boy named Melvin up here but he done stood me up. What's your name?"

"Chief Reddy," he said.

"That's a funny name. Would you stand me up like Melvin, Chief Reddy?"

"You could, could come live at my house," the boy said. "I mean on my street. There's some empty places and my great uncle is rich an' he'd pay your rent if I asked him to."

The girl frowned. Chief's heart was beating fast.

"And what would I have to do?" she asked.

"Talk to me when I was feeling sad," he said. "We could take a walk now and then."

Her name was Rhonda McKinney and there was no special light in her. Chief thought she was the most beautiful woman in the world. And even though he had thousands of years of godly experience packed into his soul, he would have given it all away for her to kiss his lips.

"You want me to take you home to your house?" Rhonda asked.

ON THE BUS ride Chief told Rhonda about his life as if it weren't tinged by immortality.

"I'm a street preacher," he told her. "I talk an' my uncle collects money. There's this guy named Hank who keeps people from jumpin' all ovah me."

"It's like you was in church but only in the street?" Rhonda asked.

"Will you marry me, Rhonda McKinney?" he answered.

She kissed his lips lightly and said, "Let's wait till you grow up some and then we'll see."

FIFTEEN

"*. . . YOU CAN SLEEP* in my bed until then," the boy was telling Rhonda that afternoon in the living room at his mother's half-house.

"Where you gonna sleep?"

"I sleep in the backyard," he said.

"On the ground?"

"On the grass and earth."

"Why you do that?"

They were sitting at opposite ends of the coral-colored sofa. Mary was in the kitchen while Nosome sat in the backyard and Henry loitered around out front. The structure of their lives had taken on a military cast. Chief realized this but what struck him was Rhonda's question.

No one else asked why he did things or what he meant when he spoke. They felt his cold fire and exulted in a world that they had always hoped for. But they didn't see the boy who had lain in his bed for years with no hope of ever even holding a water glass to his lips without help.

"It's because . . ." he said. "It's because I need to stay close to the earth. You can't understand the sky unless you can feel the ground under your feet."

"You silly. An' here I thought you was tryin' to trick me into your bed, but instead you ackin' like a preacher. Do preachers even like girls?"

"Yes. Yes we do."

"I bet you good at it, too, huh?"

"What?"

"Bein' a preacher, fool," Rhonda said nicely, giggling a little.

Chief Reddy could see that his inexperience was as deep and important to Rhonda as her presence was to him. Her eyes tightened and she clasped her arms around her middle.

"Mama always sayin' that if it wasn't for me that she would just go on back to Texas an' live wit' her fam'ly down there. Is yo' uncle really gonna pay my rent? 'Cause you know I could get some kinda job after while."

". . . Now LISTEN HERE, JUNIOR," Nosome Blane was saying at the dinner table that night, "you cain't be runnin' off like that no mo'. Your mama just about went crazy when she fount you gone."

"You know I have to do things sometimes Uncle 'Some," the boy said. "You *know* it."

Nosome opened his mouth to say something but no words came out.

"An' you cain't keep bringin' people to stay here neither," Mary said. "We already got four people under half a roof."

"The Rodriguez family next door agreed to move into an apartment down the street," Chief said, "so that Rhonda could have a place here next to us."

"What?" Mary uttered.

"They real nice people," Rhonda said as if the gift was small and insignificant. "I'ma stay in Junior's room until they move out. But I promise not to get in the way."

Chief loved how Rhonda accepted things with no wonder or affect. She took what was offered with little humility, but neither did she evince a sense of privilege.

Mary didn't like Rhonda, Chief could see that as a hot red flash in her aura whenever she caught sight of the girl. But his mother had come to see her son as the man of the house now, and even though that was not yet true, it kept her from open hostilities.

That night the boy had the most peaceful rest of his life either before, or after.

"WAKE UP," RHONDA said.

Chief knew that she would be kneeling by his side looking down on him as she had done in the park.

"There was a little gray rabbit so skinny that you would'a thought he was a monkey if it wasn't for his long ears," she said. "He was sleepin' right up next to your arm. And when I came out an' knelt down next to you, he raised his head an' looked at me an' then he went back to sleep."

"Where is he now?"

"When you moved he run away. It was like he was guardin' you until you woke up an' then the spell was broken an' he was wild again."

"Did that scare you?"

"Why I wanna be scared of a li'l ole rabbit? It was cute."

"But you never saw anything like that before, have you?"

"Stand up," Rhonda said.

Chief stood and Rhonda appraised him.

"You bigger," she said with a sneer of satisfaction. "I think you met me an' now you tryin' to catch up so I could be your girlfriend."

It was probably then that Chief Reddy knew that he was in love. He wanted to grow, was growing for her. His arms were thicker and his clothes felt tight.

"We're going to Will Roger's Park today," he said. "I'm speaking to people who have something special that we can use. You wanna come?"

"Okay. Is it around here?"

"No. Down by the ocean."

THERE WAS A LARGE GRASS field deep inside the park. Nearly a hundred of those that Chief had identified as *potentials* had been tapped by Nosome and asked to meet him there on that day.

Chief hid behind a stand of young pines while his acolytes arranged themselves before a large flat stone that the boy intended to use as his dais.

Nosome came back to give him the high sign and just

before he went out Rhonda kissed his lips, pressing her tongue into his mouth. The pleasure of that kiss dimmed even the second light of the gods. Chief inhaled and forgot for a moment how to continue the cycle of breathing.

"Go on now," she said with a smile. "Go show them people that you my man."

And so when Chief Reddy ascended the flat stone he was a little off his game. He had never been kissed like that. He had never felt about a woman as he did about Rhonda McKinney.

"I'm glad you could make it," the boy said in a cracking two-toned adolescent voice. "You hold within your minds and hearts a hope that even the gods dare not utter." His equilibrium was quickly returning. "We are all servants of the flame and you, each one of you, burn brightest among all those I have met. You've seen it in your everyday lives. Bosses give you promotions when you're no better than other workers on the same job. People fall in love with you when there are others more beautiful or suitable, richer or more worthy. They listen to you and defer to you. They dream about you but never say so.

"This is because you are holders of the flame. You burn brighter and they wish to be near that warmth.

"You have the ability not only to learn and act but also to teach. Your words, even if you do not understand their meaning, will fan the flames in the thousands and millions and your sermons will bring a revolution of awareness to the streets and into the homes, the hearts and souls of man. It is time for you to go out in the world and spread the knowledge you have gotten from me. Tell them how it felt, where the flame resides in your body. Speak from street corners and jail cells, on coffee breaks and at schools. Keep moving from place to place and tell those who live in darkness about me. Tell them that I'm coming. You will prepare them for the greater transition.

"And when you come across people like yourselves, people with the old flame of Prometheus in their breasts, take them aside and tutor them. Spread the word around the world.

"And when those you address turn away from you do not despair. They will have heard your message and it will grow in them. You are setting fires all around the fortifications that keep us from our will . . ."

It was a bright day and Chief Reddy felt power behind his words. The congregation of light-riddled men and women somehow brought out the strength in him. His heart pounded and the flames before him grew bright, illuminating even the daylight, making everything clear and knowable.

Chief knew that these nearly enlightened followers could see a world beyond the limitations of their kin . . .

And then it was as if a shadow fell, not on the light of the sun but over the illumination of the secret world that went unnoticed in plain sight. Everyone was aware of the shift in consciousness. They turned as one to the back of the crowd and saw the four men advancing.

Though Chief had never met him, he recognized Luther Unty, the leader of the uncouth men. They were at the far end of the field, but Chief could see them all, especially Luther, in bold relief and great amplification. And as the angry, powerful man approached the young leader, Chief Reddy was learning.

He perceived in the perverted darkness and light of the young thug the twisting of the fire that was the First Gift. Prometheus had tried to bestow second knowledge on this young man, but instead he awoke the potential for evil, self-loathing, and the desire to destroy. Luther Unty was the polar opposite of Chief Reddy.

Chief realized, even as Unty yelled and he and his thugs began a mad dash at the rock podium, that it was possible to awaken this malevolent force in others; that Harold Timmons, evil as he had been, now had the potential for greater devilment since gazing into the eyes Chief had inherited from the Titan.

The four black men, apocalyptic in their demeanor and rage, ran quickly, but time passed slowly in Chief's mind. Henry Minter and Nosome Blane had moved to his sides. The congregation girded themselves for the impact of the four. And Chief was wondering if the ghost of Prometheus had appeared to Unty telling him about the meeting so that the holder of the flame would not make a false move.

Unty had reached the crowd by then. He grabbed a woman and threw her twenty feet. He chopped another man dead with a single blow.

Chief concentrated with his might and time slowed until it almost stopped. He could see that Unty and his cohorts had built great strength, that they could kill everyone in that field given time.

In the well of his heart and the height of his mind Chief Reddy allowed his own energy to grow. He called upon the flames inside him using the alien song of Ma'at and then prepared to let time flow again.

"Separate them!" he shouted and then led the headlong race toward the onetime gangbanger and his crew. Henry Minter was with him. Nosome Blane was with him. A few of the men and women within earshot followed quickly. Minter hit the man on the left and Uncle 'Some took the one on the right. Chief leaped upon Luther Unty pitting his lean boy-limbs against the huge muscles of the killer while three of his acolytes did their best to restrain the fourth man.

The congregation moved out into a wide circle obeying an unspoken command. They watched as Nosome climbed on his quarry's back deftly avoiding his blows. They watched Henry and his equally powerful opponent trade blows that would have laid low a heavyweight boxer in his prime. They watched as pitifully small Chief Reddy tried to hold back the arms of his brawny adversary.

CHIEF STRAINED AGAINST Luther Unty. He felt the impossible physical strength of the man, but, at the same time, he quailed under the assault of hatred and vituperation that flowed freely from Unty's heart. The young leader could see that Unty had been feeding on hatred since his childhood in the streets. Dozens of other souls were tortured in the angry man's memories. Raped women and children, men shot down as they walked out of their homes. There were beatings and one night where he had tortured a young man just for being weak.

The malevolence in Unty's heart paralyzed Chief just as the unutterable evil of Harold Timmons had. He felt himself lose balance and fell.

"Hah!" Unty yelled as he prepared to crush Chief's head.

The young leader, at that moment, gave up the struggle thrust upon him by Destiny. He was once again a weak boy unable to rise or wipe his own ass, unable to call out and be heard. Above Unty he could see the towering semitransparent and golden image of Prometheus. The beautiful Olympian's features were somber and pensive. Once again time had slowed in Chief's mind. The respite could not save him, but only show in excruciating detail the hard-soled foot and the coming of death.

It was then that he saw Rhonda coming through the image of the Titan. She had a big rock in her hands and was intent on the head of his slayer.

Seeing Rhonda he thought about the kiss; he felt how it was to stand next to her, for her to hold him.

Everything depends on timing, he thought clearly, without fear or sense of hopelessness. This simple phrase of detached observation filled Chief with glee.

He laid there no longer prey to the pain and suffering that Unty had lived through and parsed out. It was just a matter of space and time and the flame that burned in his heart and his mind.

Rhonda slammed the big rock against the right side of Luther Unty's skull. At that moment time, for Chief, began to move quickly again. The blow to Unty's head was powerful and true but the young killer was more than proof to this attack. He swayed to the left a few inches and he lost his balance because he was only standing on one foot. He had to right himself, prepare once more to snuff out the weak child who enraged him simply by existing.

This momentary reprieve was more than enough for Chief's salvation. While Unty teetered on his feet the boy rose effortlessly, no longer paralyzed or appalled. While his friends fought doggedly, while the congregation of light watched, Unty righted himself and prepared to knock Chief down and to stomp his head and throat, balls and diaphragm. Then the killer would help his friends and they would kill as many of the followers as possible.

But before any of this could happen Chief Reddy reached out and touched Luther Unty in the center of his chest—all of the flame from his heart and mind channeling through his fingers. The concussion threw Unty backward ten feet or more, leaving him unconscious with smoke rising from his bulky dark clothes.

Luther's cohorts fell to their knees, their strength gone without Luther's hate to guide them.

Everything was still in the field. There was magic in the air but no laughter or mirth.

SIXTEEN

"*Each one of you* come forward and touch him," Chief Reddy said to his ninety-three surviving followers. "You will feel the chill of evil and desperation. You will see in him those who you cannot help to convert. Understand this feeling, hold it close, and never give the cold fire to anyone with it."

It was nighttime in the woods a few hundred yards from the first battle of Chief Reddy's life. The moon was nearly full and the young god's eyes burned brightly. Luther Unty, stripped to the waist and gagged, was lashed to a small pine. He struggled against the leather bonds made from belts donated by Redd's Revolutionaries. The followers went up one by one enduring the threats and curses that sang from the killer's muffled throat. They suffered his sickening touch and the waves of hatred that rolled off of him.

The dead had been buried and Luther's followers were tied up in a ravine not far away.

"It feel's like disease," Tana Chin said to Chief after touching Unty's forearm.

Chief placed his hand upon her brow feeling the light flow from his center into hers. In the radiance of their connection he could see Tana's children and their children and her grandparents who were born in San Francisco but never learned English very well. Her life was a gray two-dimensional background and she was an illuminated, fully formed lark flying from that bleak canvas out into the world. They smiled at each other, the boy and the fifty-something grandmother.

"I will go back to China," she said, "even though I've never been."

There was a baker and dentist, a professional burglar and two prostitutes who had come to the park, witness to their own salvation. Chief touched each of them after they had tested the evil of Luther Unty. He imparted some of himself to each and in doing so became weaker and weaker. By the time he'd addressed everyone Chief Reddy could hardly stand. When the last of his followers had gone out to spread the word he fell to his knees, the light in his eyes barely a flicker.

"I'ma kill this mothahfuckah now," Henry Minter said advancing on Unty.

"No," Chief called out from the ground where his head was being cradled by his uncle and Rhonda held his hands. "Killing him would be worse. Leave him tied to the tree. Leave him."

WHEN HE WOKE up the next morning Chief found himself on the beloved, overgrown lawn of his backyard. Hundreds of starlings were lined up on the fences and telephone lines, on the edge of roofs and the backstairs of his mother's apartment and Rhonda's new place.

"You almost died," Prometheus said.

"It felt as if I wasn't a body anymore," the boy said to the Titan kneeling beside him.

"You gave yourself to your followers," the immortal briefly named Foreman Prospect said. "They came looking for a leader but you took each one by the hand and spoke your names together. In the future you must remember never to meet with more than seventeen of your teachers at a time. Remember, Death stalks you from all sides—from above and below, and even from the people you serve."

"Did you send Unty against me?" Chief asked.

"Yes."

"Why?"

"I am dead," the Titan said simply. "I have no choice in where I go or what is seen through me. Luther Unty's hatred dragged me from the earth. I could not deny him answers to his prayers."

"And he prayed to find me?"

"Yes. But it had to happen. You will find much evil in this sundered world. Malice has grown where hope and faith once thrived. The gods have done this to your race."

"But we created the gods," Chief argued with the shimmering image.

"You have also created the poisons in the air and the ocean, the cities where no one can feel the earth or see the real sky. You have made Commerce a god that weighs on humanity like a twenty-four-pound boil on a man's back. That which is created is not necessarily good . . ."

Prometheus faded with these last words and Rhonda McKinney came out of her house wearing a sheer coral robe and no shoes.

"Come on in the house with me, baby," she said.

INSIDE SHE LET the robe fall to the floor. Chief's child's heart quailed. He was about to thank her for saving his life, maybe saving the world, but the shock of her young and voluptuous body threw all gratitude from his mind.

"Come on up in the bed with me," the older child said to the younger.

She led him into the Rodriguezes' bedroom. The family had moved in with the Joneses across the street and left their furniture for the god's girlfriend. There were religious icons everywhere: crucifixes, paintings, holy candles, and small sculptures of Mary and Jesus and the three kings.

"Take off those old clothes," Rhonda said.

When he balked she got down on one knee and began unbuttoning, then unzipping his pants. She pulled these down along with his underwear and didn't even seem to notice the straining erection.

"Get in the bed, Junior," she said as if she hadn't seen him throw a man more than twice his size ten feet with only a touch.

Chief did what she requested.

He got under the blanket but she laid out on top, her breasts and legs leaning toward him.

Chief, for his part, was silenced. The beauty of Rhonda, her courage and refusal to worship him or seek his gift sparked something in him that was unbearable and inescapable.

"I ain't gonna do nuthin' wit' you until you a big man wit' big thing for me. You hear that, Junior?"

"Aren't you afraid after what happened yesterday?" the boy asked.

"What for? I seen worse than that in my own livin' room. One time my daddy beat Mama till one'a her eyes was hangin' outta her head. You know I seen all kindsa bad shit."

"But you must have seen the power unleashed last night."

"Yeah?" she said. "So?"

"I don't know . . . can't you tell that it's different? That this is a very special moment in the history of the human race?"

"Uh-huh," she said making a sexy sneer with her left nostril and upper lip. "I always known I was special. Why else God wanna test me like that? My grandmamma told me I was somebody an' no mattah what happened I was gonna be important an' not just 'cause'a my ass neither."

Chief was momentarily aware that these times spent with Rhonda were most of the personal life he would ever have, that and a couple of stolen seconds with Uncle 'Some. He would always have these moments of clairvoyance; like when he was fighting Luther Unty and realized when he would be slain by those that feared and hated him.

"Will you become my wife?" he asked again.

"When you get bigger'n me an' got a hard on like a man,

then I'll think about," she said affecting a hard tone and a somber visage.

"I love you," Chief said and Rhonda's face softened. "The minute you got down next to me in the museum park I wanted to hold you. I've never felt like that before and won't ever again."

"That's what you say now," Rhonda said, trying to get back her hard shell.

"No," Chief said, placing his hand on her cheek. "I'm not like the others you've known or seen. My life, like yours, is fated. I have a journey and you are part of that. I love you, will never love anyone else like this."

Rhonda McKinney's breath came faster and her mouth opened. And while she wasn't phased by demons and people getting on their knees to praise Chief, she was moved by the depth of his words. Even while she couldn't have complete faith in his promises, neither could she avoid his call.

"What, what if I still say you cain't have no pussy till you the man I done wrote about in my diary?"

"Tell Uncle 'Some to buy some steaks at the Ralphs," he replied. "I have to eat a lot of meat to build back my strength and to meet your demands."

SEVENTEEN

For six days Chief remained in Rhonda's half of the family home. For three of those days she made him scrambled eggs in the morning, hamburgers for lunch, and steaks or chops at night. He ate and slept and looked upon her body feeling the blood flow and a distant call in his soul.

"You hot, baby," Rhonda said to him on the third night. "Maybe you got a fever."

"A fever for you."

It wasn't the words but the tone of voice that made Rhonda's heart skip. She reached out to touch his straining manhood but he pushed her hand away.

"Let's wait until I'm the man you need," he said.

"But you ain't grown at all. And, and I love you, Junior. I want you."

"Wait."

"*HE OKAY,*" *NOSOME BLANE* said two days later when Rhonda called him over.

"How can he be okay?" the young beauty asked angrily. "Here he hot enough to fry eggs on and I cain't wake him up. What's okay about that?"

The old man's face took on an expression that was both confused and certain.

"I don't know what to tell ya, Ron," he said. "All I know is that Foreman give me sumpin', sumpin' that let me know what's going on in Chief, in his life. I see him there. I feel his fever and I know that it's somethin' he gotta get through. It's almost ovah. He be fine in twenty-four hours."

THAT NIGHT RHONDA curled around Chief and held him despite the heat coming off his skin. She thought he was out of his head, rambling meaningless words, but in reality he was speaking in the ancient tongue, chanting the song of manhood.

Though meaningless to her, the words had a lulling effect on Rhonda's feminine character. The boy's song entered her dreams. . . .

She was standing next to a river that was very, very deep with water so clear that she could see all the way to the bottom. Huge fish with intelligent eyes moved gracefully under the surface. They were colored in reds and emerald, peach and snow white. Thousands of these behemoths traveled in the icy river. They shimmered and shone in the fast-flowing river that was filled with other life, too. Yellow crabs scuttled along the bottom while red-and-black razor fish flashed back and forth above them. Bright green birds dove for smaller fishes and a huge bear stood on the other side watching Rhonda watch the river. She wasn't afraid of the bear. She wanted to swim in the water but was worried that the beautiful fish would devour her.

Seeming to sense her dilemma, one of the regal beasts swam close to shore, near her. She was drawn to him but still nervous.

"I won't hurt you." These words came into her mind.

"But you're so big," she said.

"Come to the water's edge," the fish's words boomed in her mind.

She hesitated and then did as he said. She got down on her knees and placed one hand into the clear waters.

Suddenly the fish rose up out of the river halfway onto the bank. It dwarfed the girl. It was the size of her mother's house, larger. She fell back and was covered with a red-flecked emerald fin.

"Rise up and stroke my whiskers, girl," the fish commanded.

The white hairs flowing from the snout of the beast were soft and moist, surprisingly warm. As she rubbed his long mustache the fish vibrated and purred. He was like a kitten, she thought. Or maybe a lion tamed by a gentle touch.

"Will you ride on my back downriver?" the voice spoke in her mind . . .

————

. . . *AND, JUST WHEN* she was about to agree, a feeling came into her and she groaned with satisfaction. She opened her eyes and Chief was there caressing her, kissing her body. She reached out to touch him but the passion overwhelmed her again and she fell back in the bed crying out.

He kissed her and caressed her, pinched her thighs and pressed his fingers into her mouth.

"Come inside me, baby," she moaned. She'd never call him Junior again.

"Will you marry me?" he asked.

"What?" she cried.

"Feel me," he said.

"That's what I want, Daddy," she whimpered.

"But that will mean we'll have a child," he said. "And I cannot create life without knowing we are together."

Rhonda fell back from her lover. She reached for the lamp that was a ceramic statuette in the form of white Joseph. The bulb showed her that Chief had grown into a tall, powerfully built man who was dark-skinned perfection. His erection stood out and gave no sign of waning.

"I don't even know you, baby."

"Do you want me?"

"Yes, I do."

"Then give me your hand and I will be yours and only yours now and unto forever."

It was as if Rhonda could see the walls built around her heart being torn down by the force of his promise. She wanted to say no. She wanted to have ignored the sad boy she'd met in the park. She wanted so much and now she was at the doorway.

Finally she nodded and he made love to her the way she had always wanted. She felt that he was with her, traveling back through the pain she'd known as a child living a broken life in a broken home; as a young girl in hard streets and prison-like schools making her way among rough boys and girls who would become broken men and women like her father and the lovers that used her and then were gone.

WHEN THE SUN CAME UP Chief was ready to make love again because, even though he was now in a man's body, he was still a boy having sex for the first time.

"Hold up, baby," she said. "I need to rest."

"How long?" the boy inside the man asked.

"At least a few hours. I ain't nevah had nobody make me feel like that. I got to wait a little while or I'ma go crazy."

Chief put one hand on her outer thigh and the other against her cheek. He kissed her breasts lightly and then looked into her eyes. He knew that it was Prometheus who informed his lovemaking but he didn't care. He was also that man.

"SO WHEN YOU WANNA get married?" Rhonda asked the man of her dreams, the man who had created himself to be with her.

"We already are."

"What you mean?"

"The moment you agreed we were joined," he said. "And

now you're pregnant and we will be together with each other and through the child of our love."

"So you don't wanna get married with a judge or nuthin'?"

"Of course we can if that's what you want. I am yours in any ceremony you feel we need."

Rhonda wasn't impressed with powers of magicks, she didn't care about what other people thought or wealth, but she was moved once again by the submission of the man who was only a boy a few days before. She was going to tell him that she was his, too; that there would never be anything between them and that she would die for him no matter what he said or did.

She was about to make this declaration when the door to their bedroom broke down and six fully armed SWAT team members hurtled into the room.

PART THREE

EIGHTEEN

"On THE FLOOR!" yelled a man dressed in black battle gear, including a bulletproof vest and face mask. He was toting an automatic rifle, pointing it in Chief's face.

The newly formed young man stared at the weapon unphased but curious.

Rhonda screamed and grabbed him from behind.

The centurion-like police surrounded the bed, leveling their weapons.

"I said on the floor!" The policeman grabbed Chief by the arm and attempted to pull him from the bed, but it was like tugging on a stone statue.

"What's the problem, Officer?" the boy/man asked.

"On the floor or I will shoot!"

"Why you wanna shoot me?" Chief asked, speaking through the voice of his people. "I ain't done nuthin'. Here I am up in the bed wit' my woman an' you break down my door."

"Where's the boy!" another cop shouted.

"What boy? Me an' Rhonda's the only one's up in here."

This declaration caused three of the invaders to fan out through the bedroom and then the rest of the house. While they banged around searching for a child named Chief Reddy the man of the same name studied the ones who remained, training their rifles on him and Rhonda. He quickly discerned their names and potentials but he kept this information to himself. The serendipity of his transformation had saved him from their intentions, and he could not reveal himself.

One of the policemen was named Thornton Mead. He came from a house lined with books and parents who spent their lives dreaming about ideas, ideals, and the transition of knowledge slowly creeping across the ages like a half-frozen serpent writhing through hoarfrost toward the warmth of day. The jittering energy thrumming through Thornton's arms and legs drove him from his wistful parents and made him first a thief and then a cop. He rarely visited them, tried to keep them out of his mind. It was this attempt that made them so prominent in his thoughts.

Chief Redd closed his eyes and tried something new.

Without speaking he imagined the fire in Thornton's soul. It was weak but well formed. There was the fuel of love and hope and curiosity deep inside this man.

Breathing in through his nostrils Chief imagined himself inside the brutal young man's heart. There he planted the second flame upon the first.

Thornton shifted his shoulders and Chief knew that he had discovered a new power.

"Nobody here," a returning SWAT cop reported to the man that had wanted them on the floor.

"Out of the bed," the leader said then.

Naked both Chief and Rhonda rose and allowed themselves to be pushed and prodded into the backyard. There they were herded together with Nosome, Henry, and Mary, his mother.

Mary mother of God, Chief mused thinking of all the religious iconography in Rhonda's borrowed house. *No . . . mother of Man.*

Looking at his family Chief knew that his uncle 'Some had kept Henry from fighting back. The three were on their knees and surrounded by a dozen cops.

"Where's Chief?" Mary cried looking at Rhonda.

"He left last night," the Lover replied. "He said he needed to go out an' see the people."

Chief and Rhonda were pushed toward their little broken family. They joined them on their knees.

For a while then Chief was lost to the world of human struggle and fear. When his knees touched the overgrown, unnaturally healthy lawn he felt as if he were somehow returning home. The feel of the earth rose up through him and he groaned with the pleasure of living and having lived. His moon eyes gazed upward at the sky and were momentarily lost in their heights. Then he noticed the one thousand three hundred and seventy-four starlings that had come around to witness the trial of their master.

Chief closed his eyes and concentrated, dousing the moonlight that wanted so desperately to come out from him. In the darkness he was weightless in a cocoon made from star-ling feathers and a blue so insistent that it hurt.

"He off like the girl said, Officer," Nosome was saying. "We tried to make him heed but he's a willful boy, a pain in his poor mother's heart."

When Chief opened his eyes again he saw that the SWAT team had been somewhat mollified by the older man's words.

"And who are you?" The man who had tried to make him kneel had taken off his mask. He was asking questions in a milder tone though still he spoke like a master.

"Foreman Prospect," the boy-now-a-man replied. "I'm from Kansas. I just met Ronnie last night."

The other cop, the one whose fire Chief had kindled, was staring at him . . . wondering.

THERE WERE LOTS of questions and threats from the po-lice. At first they were looking to arrest Chief and then they threatened to arrest Mary for being an unfit mother. But finally they agreed that she would return to the station with her son or call them if she found out where he was. No-some assured them that nobody wanted wild Chief Reddy in their house. He was crazy and would be better off with the state.

"SO WHAT WE GONNA do now, Junior," Nosome asked late that afternoon in Mary Reddy's living room.

The family was there: Nosome, Rhonda, Mary, Henry Minter, and Chief.

THE GIFT OF FIRE

Mary had already yelled and screamed at Chief demanding that he tell her where her son was.

"It's me, Mama," he said over and over. But it wasn't until he allowed the spirit to fill his eyes again that she was partly convinced.

"But how can you be a man if you ain't grown inta one?" she asked her son.

"He's more of a man than the whole Marine Corps, Mrs. Reddy," Rhonda said with an emphasis that was deep and undeniable.

"WE HAVE TO LEAVE, Uncle 'Some," Chief said. "They comin' at us from all sides now. When I was lookin' at the sky today I saw a ripple."

"What kinda ripple?"

"A disturbance that means someone has come from above to destroy me. And Luther Unty is still alive and the man Harold Timmons has been sharpening his knives and perverting my flame. I can feel him searching, wanting to cut open my chest. He believes that if he can eat my heart that he will have all my power."

"And then there's the cops," Henry said.

"Yes," agreed Chief. "They want to lock me away to protect their power."

The phone ringing caused Rhonda to jump. She grabbed Chief's arm.

"It's for me," he said.

"Chief Reddy?" Thornton Mead said in the god-boy's ear.

"Yes."

"They're watching your house front and back," the soon-to-be-ex-policeman said. "Go out your side door at five to-morrow mornin'. Go into the Danby's house next door an' I will come with my truck at six-thirty. I'll get you away from them."

NINETEEN

HENRY LAY IN THE BED with Mary that night, his unnaturally strong arms around her, her eyes staring into the
luminescent blue night-light plugged into the socket.

"I used to dream that he'd come out of that room on his
own just like he did," she whispered.

"And now he's a man," Henry said. "Better."

"But I don't know what to do about him. I don't know
how to help him."

"Junior told me that you spent all day every day feedin'
him an' washin' him an' tellin' him stories. He said that he
seen you fightin' the doctors and makin' sure the nurses did
what the doctors said."

"That was only a mother fightin' for her child," she said
miserably. "But now he's like magic and Nosome is too and
so are you. All I am is just a woman. And I'm tired, Hank.
So tired I cain't even sleep."

"Don't mattah if you tired," Henry Minter, the madman, said. " 'Cause, baby, if it wasn't for you Foreman

Prospect would'a nevah been able to find Junior. He wouldn't have seen that you made a boy with a soul big enough to hold the hope of the world. All three of us, Rhonda an' me an' Nosome, got our own job to do, but you the only one already done it. You the onlyest one done proved herself. Reddy's alive an' he wakin' people up from the nightmare man done made. He woun't'a been there if you hadn't worked all them years to keep him alive."

RHONDA AND CHIEF made love through the night. For hours he massaged her with oils they found in the Rodriguezes' bathroom. She wanted to ask about how they would live, where they would go, but then she'd look at him and see that he was her ideal—a man that was strong enough to hold up the roof but who would never hit her or the child growing inside.

NOSOME BLANE LEFT the houses of his family and new friends. Since he'd been forced to give up drink he spent hours thinking about things. And thinking was a problem in a house where everybody was in love but him.

He walked a mile or so, followed at a distance by an unmarked patrol car, until he reached the house of Tonya Poundman, his sister.

He knocked and Rutherford answered the door.

"Hey, man," Nosome said to the squat and powerful carpenter.

"What you want?" Rutherford had rust-colored skin and sharp features. He looked like a man from another age who worked under a hot sun building pyramids in the jungles of South America.

"I'm glad you come back, man," Nosome said. "Nearly broke my sister's heart when you wanted her to choose."

"I said, what do you want?"

"Nosome?" Tonya called from somewhere beyond the door.

"I come to pay ya back for some'a what you done for me, Rutherford," Nosome said.

He pulled out a wrinkled, brown paper lunch bag from his jacket pocket. It was filled with something. Nosome handed the bag to Rutherford who was staring suspiciously at his brother-in-law.

Tonya came to the doorway then. She smiled seeing her brother. He smiled for her.

"What's this?" Rutherford asked.

"Seventeen thousand four hunnert ninety-two dollars an' few pennies," Nosome replied.

"Where you get it at?"

"Street ministry," Nosome said. He could feel the police watching him but that didn't matter. "Foreman used his healin' touch on Chief an' the boy been goin' around preachin' the good word."

"No healer could help that boy," Rutherford said.

"I'm just tellin' you what I know, brother. This is some'a the money the boy done made. He said he wanted his auntie to have it, for savin' me an' then for Foreman savin' him."

"You wanna come in for a drink?" Tonya asked her brother.

"I done give up the sauce, pumpkin, but I could use some water."

TWO HOURS LATER and sixteen blocks away Nosome Blane went into a bar named Tookie's Tavern. It was a place he'd frequented for a couple of dozen years back when he hadn't known more than a few minutes of sobriety a day; back when he woke up every morning and vomited before taking his first drink.

"'Some!" hailed Anita Lanan, the owner and bartender of her deceased husband's pub. "Where you been? And look at you, dressed all nice. You want a beer?"

"Naw, Nita. I done give up the sauce for a while."

"How long?" she asked with a knowing leer on her brown face.

"Not long. Just till the end of days," he said as lightly as he could. "I'll take some fizzy water though. That an' some'a them pretzels if you got 'em."

"HI," A DARK-SKINNED and handsome woman said as she pulled up a chair to Nosome's small table in the corner.

He gauged her age at forty-five but there was still the playfulness of youth in her eyes and face.

"Hello yourself," Nosome replied.

"What you drinkin'?"

"Water."

"Water an' what?"

"Just water tonight. I got some miles to travel in the mornin'," Nosome said. "What's your name?"

"Cassandra."

"An' why a pretty young thing like you wanna sit across from a old man don't have two nickels to rub together?"

The woman opened her mouth, but for some reason the words remained unspoken.

Nosome smiled.

She tried to speak four times before the words made it out. By that time she had transformed her lies into plain language.

"High yellah niggah outside give me fifty dollahs to get you drunk an' find out what you know about a boy named Chief Reddy."

"An' here I'm only drinkin' water."

"What's your name?" Cassandra asked as if starting the conversation over.

"Nosome, Nosome Blane."

"That's a funny name."

The old man shrugged his shoulders.

"What you do, Cassandra?"

"I was a ho'," she said easily, "but now I got the HIV an' you know Jesus might forgive me sellin' my body but he ain't gonna look kindly on me killin' my clientele. An' seein' that I probably be meetin' him soon I figure that I should change my ways in a hurry."

"Workin' for the cops?"

Cassandra shrugged.

Nosome ordered her a pitcher of Sangria.

———

WHEN THE PUNCH was almost gone and Cassandra and Nosome had become friends they began to talk philosophy.

"You believe in somebody live on a higher plane?" Nosome asked the ex-prostitute.

"You mean like God?"

"Exactly," the old man proclaimed. "Like God but not him the way we always known. More like our better selves, the part of our hearts that's too good for this world."

"Why the cops after you, Nosome?" she asked.

"Because I believe in that higher plane an' they worried that I might be right."

Cassandra, under the effects of the wine, squinted, trying to make sense out of the old man's words.

"They scared'a your creed?" she asked.

"You went to school huh, girl?"

"High school. Why?"

"You got to be able to read to use a word like creed when nobody already used it."

"So answer my question," she said.

"I knew a man named Foreman Prospect," Nosome spoke as if half in a trance. "He come from on top of a mountain somewhere and he had the power to touch somebody an' cure whatever it was made 'em sick—either in their soul or their body."

"Where is this man?"

"He passed on."

"Too bad. I could use a man like that."

"But he taught another man what he knew or at least some'a what he knew before he left us."

"Could this man lay hands on me," Cassandra asked, "an' cure me?"

"I haven't seen him cure nobody, but maybe he could."

"I won't tell the cops nuthin' if you ask him."

"You wouldn't tell 'em no way," Nosome said. "But you got to come wit' me tonight if you wanna see my friend. 'Cause you know by tomorrah he be gone."

CHIEF WASN'T ASLEEP when Nosome knocked on Rhonda McKinney's door. It was after one in the morning. The godboy came out wearing a pair of Henry's pants with no shirt.

"He sure look like somebody good," Cassandra said.

"He is," Rhonda said with both hunger and satisfaction in her tone. She was wearing a yellow kimono and looking more beautiful with each passing moment.

They sat in the ornate living room that had been torn up and upended by the police search. Nosome explained how he met Cassandra and what she needed from him.

As Cassandra stared at the beautiful young man she began to make out licks of flame in his eyes.

After a long time thinking Chief said, "I think I can cure you, Miss Harlow."

"How you know my last name?"

Nosome put a hand on Cassandra's wrist and she didn't pursue the question.

". . . but," Chief continued, "the cure will be painful in your heart. It will be like taking out all your secrets and all you ever did wrong and putting them in front of your mother and father in pictures, sounds, and smells that reveal everything. They will hear how you felt and what you said to the pimps and johns and women you worked with. And you won't be able to turn away. Because if you stop I will not be able to cure you and you will live on with grief in your heart.

"That's because when I heal I heal the whole person and you aren't only sick in your body. You have betrayed yourself and that needs fixing, too."

Cassandra shivered and Nosome put his arm around her. She buried her face in his shoulder and nodded.

"She ready," the old man said and Chief reached out to touch her . . .

THE WAILS THAT CAME from Cassandra Harlow were heartrending, filled with grief. Rhonda had to leave the apartment and go next door where Henry and Mary asked her what was happening.

"He doin' sumpin' to this woman Nosome knows," Rhonda said. "She done clawed off her clothes an' now she beggin'. An' if you look at her you see things . . . terrible things that she done an' seen. It makes you feel like you her mama an' you got to see her let men do awful things but you cain't stop it an' she cain't neither."

IN THE MORNING, Chief was comatose, as was Cassandra. Henry carried the heir to Prometheus through the side of the house next door and Nosome took Cassandra, limp and unwieldy as a newly deceased corpse, in his arms.

Thornton Mead came by in a locksmith's van and pulled into the neighbor's driveway where the god-boy's family loaded in and were driven away while the police sentries watched the house.

TWENTY

"YES," THE BEAUTIFUL dark-skinned minister said to the tent full of poor men and women of all colors and ages and stages of hopelessness. "There is a light inside you that grows when you work together with your neighbors, when you feed each other and heed each other and answer when your friend calls out in pain.

"Pay no attention to the men with guns in uniforms. Pay no heed when the president tells you that you must kill. Don't pay taxes but help your neighbors. Build a monument in your hearts . . ."

The Redds, as they came to be known in some places, had made it down to the outskirts of El Paso a little more than a week after escaping L.A. This was Chief's fourth sermon in six days. His practice was to walk through the town in the morning and afternoon addressing people by their names and mentioning the troubles on their minds. Those who leaned toward evil ran away but the ones who seemed like deer in oncoming headlights were handed a flyer by Uncle 'Some or Madman asking them to come to the revival meeting. Almost all who were called made the sermon if they could.

After the lecture Nosome moved through the crowd with his porkpie hat upturned for donations. Afterward refreshments were served and those who had come from curiosity spoke to each other and bonded then and there. They would leave as a group planning a new life that wasn't based on buying and selling, living in isolation or accepting hatred of the unknown as a way of life.

One or two whose light burned brighter were invited to spend a few minutes with Chief alone. He spoke to them as he had to the people in Will Rogers Park. He asked them to go out and talk to people who wanted to listen.

"There are those whose fire burns darkly," he'd always say at the end. "They will resist you and you must let them go. There is evil in the world. Many have been infected by this malady and cannot know the gift without destroying it."

"I DON'T UNDERSTAND," Cassandra said to him that night at the Crossroads Hotel at the intersection of two lonely roads that were called highways.

Everyone else was asleep when Cassandra came upon the beautiful young man sitting on a wooden crate in the half-empty asphalt parking lot. The moon was shining and Chief's eyes were on fire.

"What, Cassie?" the man-boy-god asked.

"What did you do to those people? What have you done to me?"

Chief had come outside to see the millions of stars and look for a clue to reveal his celestial pursuers. He hoped that maybe Prometheus would come to him, but after three hours of waiting Cassandra was the only one to appear.

"All my life I was confined to a bed," he said. "And then one day I was touched by something divine—"

"Like you touched me," Cassandra said.

"No, not really. I'm like a bug at the foot of the power that changed me. One day my flames might hope to reach his height. That is, if I'm not killed first."

"What's gonna happen to those people you talk to almost every night?" Cassandra asked.

"They'll go back to their homes and open their doors to each other. They'll move closer together and only one out of three will continue to work. They'll shop at the market and lay the food out on the lawn for their neighbors to come out and pick and choose what they need. They will not practice war or hatred and they will be amazed by spiders' webs and the kiss of death."

"That just sounds crazy."

"And the special ones will teach others to live outside the rancid lives they have been bunged into by meaningless labor and the codification of fear. They will have long talks in coffee shops with strangers and cousins that they've lost touch with."

"But the cops will come after them like they come after us," Cassandra argued.

"Then they will talk to their cell mates and jailors, their enemies and wardens. The prisoners will form into unions that will resist the will of retribution. After all, a man can only forgive himself, he can only truly be punished if he accepts the sin in his heart."

"But what about me, Junior?" Cassandra asked. "You did something else to me. Nosome said that you almost died when you cured my disease."

"The HIV was a little thing," he said. "It was like a wet spot that dried up instantly under the heat that you manufacture. The hard thing was the perversion of love and survival, the lies you told and the ways you made yourself ugly, hideous in the mirror. Your soul was paralyzed before you met Uncle 'Some. He awakened you and I cured you. I did this at the risk of my own life because the world needs minor deities like us. I am the Word and you, Cassandra, you are Healing. In time you can make the blind see and cancers wither. And every time you do it your life will be in the balance."

For a while the two sat in silence; the lame boy in a demigod's body with a woman who had been intimate with ten thousand men, under more stars than anyone other than Chief could count.

"What about you?" she asked after the long silence had run its course.

"Me? I like TV. I used to dream about being able to hold a glass in my own hand without dropping it. And I remember being chained to a boulder and every day an eagle would come and rip the liver from my gut."

"That's not you. You're not a TV show or a dream or a nightmare."

Chief felt the healing hand of the woman fate had brought him. She touched his face.

"I am the heir to the gods," he said without haughtiness or conceit. "They gave me powers to see and know and sometimes to offer the very beginnings of change. I have visions and now and then these revelations are not me but that from which I arise."

An electric shock ran up Cassandra's fingers but she didn't pull her hand away.

"Three hundred years ago there was a boy named Tumi captured in a raid near where men now call Ivory Coast. The boy lost his sister and mother to the king that defeated his people and he was sold to a Portuguese slave ship and chained in the hold with four hundred and twenty-seven others from different lands with different gods."

As he spoke Cassandra could see these images, smell the foul odors and also the despair.

"Tumi lost heart and after six weeks he died in his chains. He lay there open-eyed, still seeing even though he no longer breathed.

"Desire rose up in that dead soul, the desire to undo all that had been done not only to him and his people but to that king who had sold his own soul, and even to the sailors who also condemned their descendants with the mark of evil.

"I am Tumi," Chief Reddy said. "It does not matter what I ate for breakfast or why I travel from place to place setting fires in human hearts. It's not because my father abandoned me or because I broke my mother's spirit with my needs. I am nothing. Like any worker in a factory who puts the right front tire on the new car coming down the line. I'm just doing my job and nothing else matters at all."

TWENTY-ONE

A *WEEK* *LATER* Harold Timmons arrived in El Paso; drawn by the faint scent of god-spoor. He would murder one woman and devour her heart before the Community of Light, as the Redd Revolutionaries dubbed themselves in that town, became aware of him and hunted him until he had to run away. But Harold didn't care. He was after Chief Reddy's heart. He would have left anyway. Maybe he would have liked to stay long enough to eviscerate a child, but he was a practical killer. There was logic even in insanity.

WHILE *HAROLD* *RODE* buses and slaughtered hopefuls, Luther Unty was organizing youth and prison gangs around the nation. He gave wild bacchanals in empty warehouses from Spokane to Cicero, Illinois; spoke arcane verses over drugs that became more potent than anything any gang member had known before. Through his web of followers he searched for a boy-minister who could read peoples' minds and hearts.

On JULY 16 of that year, the god named Mercury stood on line in a light cotton suit to shake hands with the smirking president. When the beady-eyed plebian president looked into the dark and bottomless orbs of the messenger of the gods he said, "Don't I know you?"

"Ron Messenger, Mr. President," Mercury said. "I bring you an important piece of information."

The president stalled because long ago—before electricity and psychoanalysis, before antibiotics and Christianity— a law had been set down in Man's genes that he must listen when the messenger of the gods spoke.

The presidential handlers and the Secret Service guards tried to block the meeting set up that evening at the Wilton Hotel, but the president was adamant and Mr. Messenger was implacable.

The two sat at a table of the forty-fourth-floor bar overlooking the city of Houston. Messenger wore a black suit and a black hat with twin yellow feathers on either side of the brim.

"So where do we know each other from, Ron?" the president asked.

"I don't remember exactly," the god said, "but it was somewhere in school."

The president frowned and nodded. He wasn't sure either. So much of his early life was a blur, especially right then, when he was waging war in two countries and planning attacks on two more.

"So what was so important?" the president asked, remembering that he had a meeting with the pansy general from the Pentagon early the next morning.

"There's a young black man traveling around the country perverting the good book and turning people into enemies of democracy," Mercury said, reading key words of the shifty leader's mind. "His name is Reddy but they call him Chief Redd. Look into him and what he's done and I'm sure you'll agree that he needs to be destroyed."

"Destroyed?" the president said, finding the claim incredulous.

"Don't trust me, Mr. President. Just have the FBI or the Secret Service check him out. I'm sure you'll find that his brand of terrorism is worse than the whole Middle East combined."

The most powerful man on earth turned his head to look out on the southern city. It was night outside but he knew that the temperature was over a hundred degrees. He turned back to ask the man named Messenger about the nature of the black man's sermons, but his old friend, who he didn't really remember, was gone. . . .

MEANWHILE THE REDDY FAMILY traveled through Louisiana and Mississippi, Arkansas and Florida. When federal agents tried to infiltrate one of his meetings five miles north of Tampa, Chief and his family borrowed a mobile home from one of his advanced acolytes and drove nonstop to Oregon. There they began the sermons again. They worked their way up into Washington State and out onto the islands of the Puget Sound.

On their fourth night in the wild of the Sound Chief once again found himself sitting outside at night hoping for guidance from his creator. Before the Transition, Chief saw himself as a thing, something created and formed from the experiences of another. He had been a dreaming worm tended by his mother, too weak even to fall out of bed on his own. Now he was tall and powerful, women said that he looked like an onyx statue if the ancient Greeks had worked in that stone. He could read the light from any being and see into the dark dissipated hearts of men, but there was little to his own personality. There weren't the scars and blemishes of experience in him like there were in others. Madman, 'Some, Mary, Rhonda, and Cassandra all had deep marks on their souls, scoring that made them unique for their purpose.

But to Chief his soul seemed like that of an infant, smooth and without consequence except for the events of the past few months. He had the worries of a young child before the Titan came into his room, his world. And now he, the least among men, was their guidepost, their one hope.

Having these thoughts Chief Reddy didn't notice the two-hundred-pound timber wolf that approached from the nearby stand of pine. That morning the huge feral creature had scented the god-boy from fifty miles away. He left his pack and loped through the woods without stopping until he got to the edge of the trailer park camping grounds.

He advanced on the musing demigod both fearful and ecstatic; for wolves still remembered the gods. Wolves had their own fires and those flames burned brightly and hot. That was why animals were drawn to Chief. They came to offer their fealty.

When the boy lifted his head he was looking into the eyes of the brown and gray wolf. Before then Chief had seen the animals that followed him as curious beasts attracted to the spoor of Prometheus. But in this wild thing from the deep wood the heir of the flame felt a kinship and an answer to his innocence. The wolf gave to Chief his feral nature and his wild love of wind and scent, fresh blood and the clear notion of an eternal present.

He held out a hand and the timber wolf batted it with his long snout.

"What shall I call you, friend?" Chief asked.

Timberman. The word came into Chief's mind. He tore off his clothes then and ran with his new comrade into the woods. They ran together all night feasting on rabbits and howling at the sky.

TWENTY-TWO

"NOW WE GOT TO BE TRAVELIN' wit' a wild animal?" Mary Reddy said the next morning.

Rhonda had already made friends with the wolf. They were sitting on the ground together at the back of the mobile home. She was scratching his chest vigorously with both hands and he was licking her neck hungrily. Now and again he'd growl and leap to his feet as if realizing that he was in an alien and dangerous situation, but then he'd sniff the air and look toward Chief. The sight of the Heir calmed the wolfish fears and Timberman, as Chief dubbed him, would settle down with Rhonda again.

"He's my heart, Mama," Chief said simply.

"What's that mean? Your heart?"

"I don't know what it means, Mama. But I need him to carry something for me."

"Like a mule?" Mary, the daughter of country folk, said.

"Not something like that," the god-boy answered, trying to find an answer within his own words. He failed and turned to his Titan-appointed guardian. "Where we goin' today, Uncle 'Some?"

"Salt Lake City, Junior," Nosome Blane said. He and Cassandra had spent the night in a motel down the road. "Got some real religion up that way. Lotta people already half the way there."

ON THE RIDE Chief sat at the back of the mobile home with his arm around Rhonda and Timberman at his feet. Mary and Henry sat together further up talking about their disparate experiences; him fatherless and on the street picking fights and scrambling to survive and her waiting hand and foot on a boy she loved more than anything—a boy she now felt was lost to her, a boy whose heart was carried by a wild animal.

Nosome drove while Cassandra read to him from all kinds of different books. Cassandra, it turned out, was well educated up until the age of eighteen. She'd used books as way to escape the pain of her life. And now that she was healthy and on the road with the god-boy, her greatest pleasure was reading biographies and novels, how-to books and religious tomes to her old, old man.

Nosome for his part would drive hour after hour without getting tired or bored. He listened to every word Cassandra read, increasing his knowledge by leaps and bounds. Another thing that Foreman Prospect had done to him was to make his mind a sponge for knowledge and simple detail. He remembered every acolyte in every town in every state they drove through. Faces, street signs, passing comments by strangers in the street, Nosome even remembered errant sounds and noises. He himself was like some great tome recording all the aspects of the world.

While the old man drove and listened he'd look up into a mirror above his head now and again to see Chief in the far back on the padded bench with his wolf and his girl. Every hour or so he'd catch the alien eye of his grandnephew and spiritual guide; thus entering into the experience of the vastly expanded, and yet inexperienced, mind.

For the most part Nosome could tell that his nephew was just a boy with few experiences and little notion of all the little things in the world. The elder Blane realized that Foreman had empowered him to help guide the boy in the indispensable trivialities of life, the trace elements that bound the soul to the world. They often talked about everyday things like stoplights and jazz clubs, convenience stores and how people greeted each other on the street.

"Junior," Nosome would say, "you are the servant to man not the master."

"I know that, Uncle 'Some."

"Yeah. And I knew for forty-sumpin' years that I should get sober, but you know that didn't make me put down the bottle."

ON THE DAYS while Nosome drove and Cassandra read, when the driver would look up and see into his nephew's eyes, there often came a moment of realization that was neither person but a temporary amalgam of their altered spirits.

Nosome would ponder this experience in the dark after making love to Cassandra even though he thought that sex in his life was dead and gone.

In his thoughts Nosome would be stopping at Salt Lake City, Boise, Chicago for two weeks, and on to Minneapolis, Cleveland, and Cincinnati. They traveled through dozens of towns and rode in the mobile home using the donations of newly turned Redd Revolutionaries to buy their gas. Nosome would remember everything and Chief would see these memories in their brief connections. Life for both men was growing like a fire in the dry woods of late summer.

They traveled for only two months but it seemed, especially in those daily meetings of the mind, that they had been wandering for years in the spiritual desert of America. Through Chief's mind Nosome could see the sadness and desolation that filled the hearts of almost everyone they met.

"How can you take it, Junior?" 'Some asked his nephew at Howlin' Wolf Trailer Park, twenty-six miles outside of Memphis.

"Take what, Uncle 'Some?" the boy asked.

"All these poor people draggin' 'round they souls like hundred-pound sacks of dead fish stinkin' up everything and hardly able to take a step wit'out groanin' out loud from the strain."

It was nighttime and Chief's eyes were ablaze. He and Rhonda had just made love in a little abandoned shack in the woods. He was feeling relaxed and unconcerned about the world. Where Nosome remembered everything, Chief's mind, when he wasn't preaching, was filled by sensual pleasures brought to him by Rhonda and Timberman. The only times he was forced to think were when Nosome would look in his eyes or have a late-night talk.

"I don't like to think about the way they are, Uncle," Chief said. "I try to see 'em the way they will be when the fire takes hold and they turn their backs on the foolishness of their lives.

"In twenty years we'll come back the way we've been and whole cities will be filled with people who live for each other opening their doors and their hearts to the world before them. They won't need leaders or guards or policemen to do right. They will make a heaven right here on earth and, and when they die they'll be their own angels in a place that even I can't imagine."

Listening to Chief's answer, Nosome Blane learned something both terrible and exultant; something that was hidden between the lines of the boy's vision. Nosome was afraid because he didn't feel equal to the task that Foreman Prospect had set out for him.

"Junior," the spry old man said then.

"Yeah, Uncle 'Some?"

"I wanna ask you sumpin' 'bout what we doin'."

"What's that?" the boy said. He was thinking about Rhonda's body, how she could make him go crazy by just letting a shoulder-strap fall or a lazy finger graze his neck. Then he remembered her hitting Luther Unty with that rock even though she could have stayed hidden and run from him.

"What if Foreman wasn't arrested and put in that cell wit' me?"

Chief snapped out of his reverie and felt a slight pang of

fear. His face clouded over for a few moments and then he smiled.

"Either it happens or it don't," the boy uttered.

"Come again," 'Some said.

"Either it happens or it don't, Uncle 'Some. The world don't have no take backs. You sleepin' in a house an' the stove catch on fire. Later on you wake up in a hospital an' there's burns all ovah your body. You think, 'what if I was out when the spark flashed an' the fire grew,' but that's ovah. You in the hospital dyin' an' they ain't no way back to when you was whole." Chief realized that he was speaking the language of his uncle not of Prometheus the Titan. This seemed appropriate. He wasn't a single being like other men. He was Transcendent, made of the impossible combination of mud and sunlight.

"But we not wounded, Junior," Nosome said. "We livin' in bliss."

"Happiness has a cost, Uncle," Chief said sadly. In his heart he was saying good-bye to his childhood. He realized for reasons he did not yet fully understand that his uncle's question marked the end of innocence.

"What kinda cost?"

"By now there are seventeen thousand three hundred and twenty-four souls that have had their light reignited and the second flame placed upon that. They are forming into groups that will resist the darkness of the gods. There are eight hundred and sixteen lamplighters that have been sent out on the path to inflame many thousands more. And while the flames of the Titan grow so do our enemies. They are, even now, planning to destroy us."

"Then let's make us a army," Nosome said. "Let's settle down in New York or L.A. and convert us a army to hold back thems that wants to kill you."

"I could do that but then the Word I'm giving would become like Luther Unty and worse—Harold Timmons. The army I'd raise would never seek peace and civility. No, Uncle, I can only do what I'm doing just like we cannot escape the fate pressed upon us by the Titan."

"Why you talk one way sometimes and then another way a few minutes later?" 'Some asked as a way of accepting Chief's decree.

"Because I'm just the vessel, the glass that holds the wine."

"I cain't drink wine no mo'," Nosome said.

The boy laughed as his uncle shook his head ruefully. The talk, Nosome knew, was over . . . but the trouble was just beginning.

TWENTY-THREE

*T*HEY ARRIVED ON BEALE STREET that noon after having parked their vehicle on an empty lot five miles away. Nosome wanted to do the sermon on the outskirts of town but Henry "Madman" Minter wanted to do their work on the street of musicians because Chief had predicted that his father, Terrence, would be there.

"He's been freed from prison," the young cult leader had said. "But he is crippled and near death."

*C*HIEF WAS AMAZED at the lights that blazed in the musicians' hearts and souls on that street. The spirit of Prometheus was emboldened by the possibilities he saw among the people there.

Chief called out their names and they followed him down the sidewalks playing instruments and humming tunes that had been sung in men's hearts since the days before the printing press and even the loom.

RON MESSENGER ARRIVED at the Memphis Airport at
6:15 that morning with a friend of his named Bill Archer.
Archer had come from the same place as Messenger and
was now in the employ of a covert branch of special services. On Olympus Archer was known as Phoebus, a member of Zeus's elite guard. He was armed with a long-range
hunting rifle that had no telescopic site or any other kind
of aiming mechanism.

"I could shoot a gnat off of a fly's ass from two miles
away," Archer had said to the shifty-eyed president. "I was
formed from the ideal of the hunt."

"Huh?" the president, who looked short but was decep-
tively tall, said.

"He's a born hunter," Ron Messenger said. "That's all he
means, Mr. President."

"Does he understand that we need this done clean and
neat with no strings, no trail to follah?"

"He's the best, sir," the god said. "Once the job is done
he will be gone and not the whole of the FBI will find even
a footprint behind him."

"I'm not sure," the president said, hesitating.

They were standing in an empty hangar at the farthest end
of an abandoned airport twenty miles north of Baltimore.

"You checked this Chief Reddy out, haven't you?" Messenger asked.

The shifty-eyed president stared at this man he remembered so well and yet hardly knew. He wondered, not for
the first time, why he felt compelled to believe his words.

"People are cutting themselves off from their governments and their peoples," Messenger said. "They aren't paying taxes and most of them aren't even going to their jobs anymore. They're working against your policies, sir, and there are more of them every day."

"But he has so many followers," the president argued. "What difference would killing him make now?"

"He is the heart and soul of the movement, sir," Messenger said. "His demise will break the heart in them."

Mercury neglected to say that a special team was, even at that moment, forming on Olympus; a team that would come to earth and kill or pervert all of Chief's followers. It's what they did with Prometheus's first gift of flame.

"No trail?" the president asked.

"Not one clue, sir."

TIMBERMAN WAS LEFT in the van when Chief and his friends departed for Beale Street. But the feral beast tore through the flooring of the mobile home and stealthily made his way after a scent only he could discern.

BEALE STREET WAS ALIVE with music and dancing, free-flowing libations and the words of the god-boy.

"You are my people," Chief Reddy said aloud. Everyone everywhere in a two-block radius could hear the words in their minds. "There is no reason in war. There is not satisfaction in revenge. There is no god sitting on any throne without you tilling the earth and carving from stone and giving birth again and again. There is no reason to lie or elevate yourselves above your station because you are all a part of divinity. There is no thing that will make you better—no gold or jewel or piece of paper saying you own anything but your own body and your own joy. There is no you without the person standing next to you. There is no other way to live. . . ."

While he preached tubas boomed and trumpets blared, women cried and men did, too. While he exhorted them with words they already suspected they sang and danced and absorbed wisdom that had lain dormant in Man's soul for uncounted generations.

AT THE EDGE of the huge crowd of revelers Henry Minter saw an old man in a wheelchair gazing blissfully in his direction. Henry was supposed to be standing next to Chief but he sensed something and slowly drifted away.

"Are you Terry Minter?" Henry asked the old man.

"Yes, I am. Do I know you?"

"I'm Henry . . . your son."

TWILIGHT WAS COMING on and Bill Archer moved across the roofs above Beale Street with inhuman agility and extreme focus. No one saw him. No one was looking for him. The people in the streets were having the celebration that they had been waiting for for well over a thousand years. The prophet had come and they were him. His words were their hearts. His life was their hope.

———

*M*ARY SCANNED THE CROWD for Madman. Nosome was worried but not exactly sure why. Chief stood on the roof of a baby blue Ford Explorer exhorting the crowd and feeling for the first time his soul rising up out of his body.

When he looked down upon the thousands that filled the streets, dancing and making music, he saw in a third-floor window the glittering image of Prometheus. The Titan waved—good-bye?

*A*T THAT MOMENT Timberman leaped through the air while Bill Archer pulled the trigger of his gun. Nosome Blane looked up to see the wolf tearing out a man's throat on a rooftop and then he heard the men shout and the women scream. He turned to see Chief hanging off the side of the SUV, his head oozing blood.

Somewhere Henry Minter was running. A wolf howled its lament over the crowd's cries. Cassandra ran to help but life was gone from the man who had ripped contagion from her—body and soul.

On the rooftop Phoebus looked up at the darkening sky, experiencing real death and cursing his fate.

In a small nearby store Nosome found five cans of lighter fluid. And while the Redd Family held back the crowd he drenched the dead god-boy and set him afire.

The flames leaped high into the night and expressed images that everyone could see. The music was over. The celebration was done. Somewhere a wolf howled and Hope had died . . . but not without leaving its legacy.

The flames were beautiful and anyone who saw them could not grieve for long because the inferno that was Chief Reddy's body lit up the night and the hearts of Memphis. Blacks and whites and browns and every other color and persuasion of men and women and children came out of their houses to be inspired to live, for that same flame now blazed within them.

Mary and Rhonda mourned the son and the lover. Nosome fell to his knees and prayed. Henry Minter ripped at his breast and Cassandra held him, filling his anguish with the restorative spirit that Chief had given her.

Ron messenger, upon seeing the flames rise up above the buildings on Beale Street, was deeply wounded by the power and content of the fire. He ran away through the oncoming crowds cursing Prometheus, who had given his only friend, Nosome Blane, the knowledge to keep the flame of the gods alive even as their herald perished.

Nor was the flame soon over. Fueled by the divinity of Chief Reddy's body the blaze grew hotter and hotter. Nearby buildings began to burn and the crowd moved into wider and wider circles away from harm, but not so far as to distance themselves from the Light and the Heat of their deliverance.

Fifty-seven city blocks were leveled by the heat before the dawn had come. Stone buildings collapsed. Cars melted into slag where they stood. Sidewalks and asphalt streets turned molten tar and stone. People from hundreds of miles around came to bask in the curative balm of light. Reds and blues, ochres and violet shimmering lights cascaded down upon the citizens of Chief Reddy's new world.

Bill Archer's body was reduced to ash anointing the new age.

Mercury returned to heaven scorched and bleeding from the god-child's fire.

Luther Unty awoke in a Gary, Indiana, crack house choking on smoke that he couldn't locate.

Harold Timmons was preparing to cut the heart out of a child he had taken out from her bed when the room started spinning and he fell unconscious. When he awoke the police had arrested him for a dozen major crimes.

NO ONE NOTICED the three women, two men, and one sad wolf that fled the flames they knew too well. Behind them they left the devastation of enlightenment. And though fully a million citizens were transformed and elevated by the light, many dark hearts failed that night. Men and women who were formed by evil were sundered and their souls drifted down to Hades. And hope was born the way Chief had imagined it.

EPILOGUE

A YEAR LATER and a million citizens of Memphis had gone out into the greater world: ragged flames of hope and inspiration spread around the globe intent on igniting a movement for unity.

Luther Unty worked to undermine the greater cause. His powers were increased by Vulcan and Dionysus, but the gods feared that their rule was over.

Harold Timmons mastered his fellow prisoners and sent them out to do his evil bidding. From his cell he ordered crimes that would decimate many thousands of the Redd Revolutionaries.

The shifty-eyed president ordered every person who wore red and preached on street corners to be surveiled and arrested under the second Patriot Act.

Everywhere people were coming out of their houses to hear the ministries of those who saw the fire that leveled so much of Memphis. Bands played all over the world and even though hundreds were slaughtered by frightened presidents and dictators, holy men and criminals, thousands more arose to carry on the Word.

ON THE ANNIVERSARY of the death of Chief Reddy, Nosome Blane called together Mary, Henry, Rhonda, Cassandra, and the wolf Timberman. They met at the rock in Will Rogers Park. They were a sad lot. Mary had left Henry as, she believed, he had abandoned Chief. Madman fell back into his old ways wandering the streets and drinking. Cassandra also went homeless and Rhonda bore a child, a son she named Truth. They lived in the old mobile home, and though she loved her son Rhonda was rarely known to smile.

"WE HAVE COME here to remember, Junior," Nosome said. "Now I know that you all hurtin' and sore and maybe even you blame each other and yourselves for the boy's death. But you know he wouldn't want that. He would want you to get together again and remember him for what he did to this world . . . for what he's doin' every day. And so I want you all to gather 'round this stone where he taught his first teachers and here we will remember him."

Mary moved away from Henry, who was drunk or high, but Cassandra drew him into the circle. Rhonda, her baby in her arms, smiled briefly and took her place at the memorial stone. Timberman leaped up onto the flat rock and curled down, a wolven way to show respect.

Nosome Blane lifted his arms to the sky and exhorted

the spirit of mankind to witness the ceremony of remembrance.

"We want to remember Junior here today in the place where he proved that he was a man," Nosome said. "We want to stand here as a family at least one more time and deny the powers that would keep us as their slaves. We want to call up the light and the fire that that boy brought to us without ever questioning his fate or his own needs. There's a revolution goin' on out there. There's a war for peace bein' waged in Asia and Europe, Africa and right here in the streets of Los Angeles. There's a battle ragin' an' because Junior never shirked or flinched the war is being won. I call now on the fire of my friend Foreman Prospect. I call on it to show itself to us here so that we can see where Junior wanted us to go. . . ."

"Look!" Mary shouted, pointing at the midsection of the couching wolf.

Smoke and then flame rose from the thick and shaggy brown and gray pelt of the huge canine, but he didn't whimper or even seem to notice. The fire jumped high in the air, covering every color seen and not seen by the naked eye.

When the fire rose above them all the Redd Clan gazed upon it each in their own commune with the flame. The wolf's body dissipated, feeding the memorial fires. Mary crossed over to Henry and embraced him. A broad grin showed itself on Mary's visage. Again, Nosome Blane fell to his knees.

Cassandra took a step toward the fire. If anyone had witnessed this movement they would have seen that the woman left an image of herself, the whore and drug addict, behind like the empty husk of a butterfly cocoon or snake. She reached into the fire and drew out the form of a beautiful naked man with a wolf cub in his arms. One of his eyes became the flame that had engulfed him while the other shone like a half-moon at midnight.

"Thank you," Chief Reddy said. "I have traveled a long, long way to get here. Now it's time for us to move."

On the Head of a Pin

ALSO BY WALTER MOSLEY

WALTER MOSLEY

CROSSTOWN TO OBLIVION

On the Head of a Pin

TOR®

A TOM DOHERTY ASSOCIATES BOOK • NEW YORK

On the Head of a Pin

I WAS WORKING AT Jennings-Tremont Enterprises (JTE) when Ana Fried and, I suppose, the rest of us, quite by accident, happened upon the most important discovery in the history of this world, or the next.

JTE's primary work was developing advanced animatronic editing techniques for film. It was our job, or at least the job of the scientists and programmers, to develop animation tools that would create high-end movies indistinguishable from live action.

Joseph Jennings's childhood dream was to make new movies with old-time stars. He wanted Humphrey Bogart and Peter Lorre side by side with Rudolph Valentino, Myrna Loy, Marlon Brando, and Natalie Portman. These new *classics*, he envisioned, could be made in small laboratories by purely technical means. Had we been successful, the stock in JTE would have been worth billions. Instead, we were secretly vilified, physically quarantined, and warned, under threat of death, not to create documents such as this one. Writing this memoir, my second act of true rebellion, is necessary in spite of the danger because there must be some record of what really transpired in case the government gets to me before the Alto arrive.

But I don't want to get ahead of myself.

My name is Joshua Winterland. I suppose you could call

me a failed writer. Failed is a harsh word but valid in this case, because all my life I wanted to be a playwright. I've written thirty-seven plays that have each been rejected by every theater, playwriting competition, and creative writing school in the country.

I am thirty-nine years old and have been writing since the age of nine.

When I realized that I'd never be successful, or even produced, as a playwright I began work as a technical writer for a succession of various companies and institutions in California's Silicon Valley. I was the guy who wrote the manuals for new hard- and software. My day's work was to help consumers figure out what tab to hit and where to look up the serial number, how to register online or over the telephone, and what safety precautions to take before turning on a new system.

My fate was recast when the country went into a serious economic recession and, coincidentally, my girlfriend, Lena Berston, woke up one day to realize that she was in love with my childhood friend Ralph Tracer.

Lena told me one morning, before I was off to work at Interdyne, that Ralph had called because he was coming in from San Francisco that evening and she had offered to cook dinner for the three of us. I thought this was odd because Lena rarely cooked on weeknights, and she had always said that Ralph wasn't *her kind of person.*

"It's not that I don't like him," she'd said more than once, "but he just doesn't interest me."

I didn't give it any serious thought. Ralph was a good guy. I'd known him since junior high school in Oakland.

He was from a different neighborhood but we made an early bond. We'd talked to each other at least once a week since I was thirteen years old, sharing our boyhood dreams. I planned to be a playwright and he wanted, in the worst way, to lose his virginity.

Our goals alone spoke volumes about the value of reduced expectations.

WHEN I GOT HOME Ralph was already there sitting at the kitchen table. Lena was cooking. I felt proud that she was my girlfriend and that she was wearing her sexy, rainbow-colored, short skirt. Between the two of us Ralph had always been the ladies man. I had spent most of my life between girlfriends, and so being with Lena made me feel very, very good.

Don't get me wrong . . . I really liked her as a person. If you had asked me at any time before that last dinner I would have told you that I loved her. But after what happened that love got lost and I can no longer speak for it.

"Lena and I have something that we need to talk to you about, buddy," Ralph said in the lull between the soup and the rack of lamb.

"What's that?" the fool asked.

When I glanced at Lena she turned away, but still I didn't get the message. It's amazing how human nature creates the feeling of security for itself, believing in a world that might cease to exist at any moment—might already be gone.

"I didn't mean for this to happen," Lena said, forcing herself to look me in the eye.

She had come back to the table without the meat. This I took as a bad sign.

"Lena was up in San Francisco," Ralph was saying. "I'd told her that I knew the curator of modern art at the Freierson Museum."

"Yeah. I remember."

"She came by the house and I offered her a drink. That's all."

"That was nine months ago," I said, thinking of all the nights in the last nine months when Lena had been too tired to make love.

"We tried to stop, Josh," Lena said. "Every time I went to see Ralphie I swore I'd never do it again. But . . ."

Ralphie.

"We didn't mean to hurt you, buddy," my onetime friend said.

They both talked more. I can remember words but not the ideas or concepts they formed. I listened politely for maybe a dozen minutes before standing up. Ralph, I remember, got to his feet, too. Maybe he thought I was going to hit him. I don't know.

I took my jacket from the hook on the wall and walked out of the house. Lena, to her credit, followed and pleaded with me. I think she said that they would leave the house for me to live in. I'm not sure. I drove off and stayed at a motel that night. In the morning, nineteen minutes after I'd gotten to work, I was informed that Interdyne had gone out of business due to a dip in the stock market the night before.

The motel was called the Horseshoe Inn. It cost sixty-

four dollars a night to stay there (plus tax and county fees). I went to thirty-six tech labs in the area over the next five business days; no one was hiring and many were laying people off.

That Wednesday I drove down to L.A., bought a newspaper in Beverly Hills, and applied for a job at JTE Labs in Redondo Beach. Being a California company, and therefore at least partially New Age, they wanted to hire a writer to record the progress of their research, a kind of Have Memoir Will Travel. I was to use video cameras, a computer journal, and even pen and paper in a pinch. Once every two weeks I interviewed all the nineteen employees, myself, and the boss—Joe Jennings.

That's really why I'm risking my life creating this document; just in case my plans fall short. It was my job, my only purpose, to record this story. And seeing that the content is of monumental importance I cannot allow special interests, government institutions, and/or religious bodies to stop the advancement of science.

I STOPPED WRITING for a while after the last word of the previous sentence because I can't vouch for its veracity. The idea that we're dealing with science was at best an assumption on our part. And not all of us at that. Cosmo Campobasso believed that the Sail (which is as much his creation as anyone else's) was a window to God. He wouldn't have used those words—he called the Sail the Blank Page and believed that he saw Mother Mary standing next to me on a Santa Monica rooftop.

Cosmo was an unschooled immigrant from the Sunnino Mountains of the Molise region of southern Italy. A craftsman, he wove the nine-by-twelve-foot fiber-optic tapestry that is the Blank Page, the Sail. The millions of spiderweb-thin strands were meticulously interlaced by the barely educated artisan over a six-year period.

Every morning when I got in, big, lumpy Cosmo had already been there for hours pulling the nearly invisible strands across the broad loom. The Page, as it grew, was a gossamer, semiopaque, and diaphanous fabric that rippled and flowed on its cherry wood, lead-fretted frame. The care that Cosmo exhibited was more than any man of the modern age would have been able to sustain. His assistant, Hampton Briggs of Watts, took the ends of each strand and connected them to one of the sixteen motherboards that were suspended around the growing tapestry. These millions of connective strands glistened in the space around the floating, nacreous Page.

The Page Room, as it was called by some, was an old airplane hangar from the 1930s set on property that JT Enterprises bought at auction when the previous owners, inept real estate speculators, went into bankruptcy. The Blank Page looked to me like the sail on a small schooner, picking up breezes that seemed to come from another dimension, hovering above the corroded concrete floor like a mortal's unconscious dream of divinity. I'm no scientist but I've been told that the places where the minute fiber-optic strands intersected cause an entry in the computer system that it was connected to. This entry is a bit of data that could be manipulated as far as hue, intensity, and texture.

And even though very little energy passed through the Page, a strong light from behind was designed to bring out the images wrought by JTE's copyrighted software.

These tiny intersections were created not only by their proximity but also by Cosmo's impressing them with two tiny silver rollers that he created after being told by Ana Fried what was necessary for the computer system.

There was some speculation toward the end there that the frets of lead and silver rollers had an impact on the final outcome of the Sail. This conjecture reveals the underlying spiritual questions about the project and its miraculous output.

"WHAT WE ARE doing here," diminutive, sixty-one-year-old Ana Fried told my camera at an early stage of my position as Company Scribe, "is re-creating reality. Within ten years I will be able to generate a film of you at the battle of Appomattox, or among the onlookers at Caesar's assassination. No one will be able to tell the difference between reality and our images."

"What will be the applications of this new software?" I asked, sitting, as always, off camera.

"We will be one step down from the Creator," she said, her olive-hued face tightening into an expression that she considered dramatic. "Imagining a world and then making it."

TODD PINKUS SAID to my camera that "Everybody from schoolteachers to forensic investigators will be able to use these tools to enhance their jobs."

"What about criminals and propagandists?" I asked.

I didn't like Todd.

Pinkus frowned at the question. He was a thin, very white man with wire-rimmed glasses that were too big for his face. His walnut and gray hairline was receding and his lips had no thickness to them at all.

"Questions like that are designed to retard growth, not augment it, Josh. The question you should have asked was how would these tools benefit the policeman and the lecturer?"

"You're a programmer right?" I replied.

"I'm the senior programmer-analyst on this project."

"And I'm the project's memoirist. So I get to ask the questions."

Pinkus winced as he considered his reply. He didn't like me from the first day, didn't like the fact of my job. He was the kind of guy who thought he knew everything—and that the world orbited this knowledge. If he had been a heart doctor and you came to him with the early signs of cancer, he would have prescribed blood pressure medicine and suggested a bypass.

"The problem with your people, Josh," Pinkus replied, "is that you have never raised yourselves out of the nineteenth century. Slavery is over and all the possibility in the world waits outside your door."

By *my people* Pinkus was referring to those that are commonly called African American. I only mention that here because he believed that my dislike of him was a direct reflection of his feelings toward me. He believed that my aversion to him was about race when in actuality I was only

disgusted by his arrogance and pomposity—leaving it to him to be offended by skin color.

"So you believe that I and *my people* are still living in slavery?" I asked.

"What does that have to do with the project?"

"My job is to record, for Posterity, the moods, characters, and jobs of the people that have created this revolutionary system. A hundred years from now you will be some of the most famous technicians in history. Imagine if we could know as much about the designers of the pyramids?"

"I refuse to participate," Todd Pinkus said. He made a motion as if he were going to stand and leave.

"You know that Joe Jennings views these tapes every month," I said, my tone just a wee bit threatening.

The hatred in Pinkus's eyes was a balm to my emotional wounds. For what I couldn't do to Ralph Tracer, Todd Pinkus would stand in effigy.

He settled back into the chair in my jury-rigged interview room.

"Can we go on?" he asked.

"Will you let me do my job?"

"Of course. I wasn't trying to take your job I was just . . . never mind. Go on. Ask me whatever."

DOCUMENTING THE BLANK PAGE project was just what I needed to get over Lena and Ralph and the impact the recession was having on most Americans. I worked sometimes as much as twelve hours a day, six days a week . . . and JTE paid time and a half overtime.

My hours were so long because people worked nearly round the clock on the Blank Page project. I could walk in at almost any time of the day or night and have someone to interview. That's how I, at least in the Band-Aid sense, overcame the last emotional hurdle of Lena's betrayal.

Doreen Howard was Todd Pinkus's boss. She was the systems analyst who envisioned the underlying symphony of the animation project. Doreen was a wasp-waisted, bottle-blond, forty-something bombshell. Her lips were too red and her breasts impossible. There was something coarse about her beauty. You would expect to see her slinging pancakes at an IHOP rather than designing the Lifelike Imaging Process at JTE. Regardless, Doreen was some kind of genius. She'd never been to college but she'd worked in computer animation since the age of seventeen.

"I took to hexadecimal like crap to the sewer," she told me on our first interview.

All of our interviews were colorful like that. I think she could tell how grateful I was for her candid and lively talks.

One evening we were discussing the amount of work she orchestrated using Pinkus and a dozen Indian programmers in Mumbai. She explained how boxes of infinitely re-iterated logic appeared in her mind and were then assigned to the appropriate drone.

"I think of my programmers as drones," she said. "They're like the boxes of logic and pages of design. And I see myself as queen bee organizing the material into an infinity of images."

Doreen was looking into my eyes as she spoke. It wasn't

until I felt a bead of sweat rolling down my back that I understood the effect her words were having on me.

Just at that moment of awareness she said, "Turn off the camera, Josh."

I did so.

"That's how I see the world," she said, sitting back in the red lacquer chair I used for my subjects. Her dress was wide and light blue, the hem, when she was standing, came down to mid-calf. It was the classic farm girl's dress, but it wasn't dowdy on her.

"How's that?" I asked, trying to keep myself from choking.

"Drones."

"Uh," I articulated.

"Would you like to follow me home so I could show you?"

SEX WITH DOREEN HOWARD was the simplest and most gratifying physical experience I'd ever had. She brought me in, wrung me out, and sent me packing in three hours flat. When I got home I fell asleep without a thought in my head, and the next day, when Doreen and I ran into each other in the small company cafeteria, we smiled and said hello as if there was no last night . . . or tomorrow.

Doreen, as she said, was queen and so I never initiated with her. Now and again, every few weeks or so, she'd ask me what I was doing that night. If I had plans I canceled them, but usually I didn't have much to do outside of work.

I lived in a two-room bungalow behind a big yellow house at the base of the Hollywood Hills. There I watched TV and slept—never dreaming that I was on the cusp of the enlightenment of the ages.

DON'T GET ME wrong, Doreen wasn't cold or heartless. She just saw most of the world as building blocks in her playroom. The operant word there is *most*. Doreen had a heart. And that heart could be pierced.

Langly Banner, lead singer in a Hollywood rock band called Bad Intentions Inc., took Doreen home one night and kept her there for three months. He had long black hair and a thin but powerful frame. He sang full out when he was on stage at the Whiskey or House of Blues. Doreen went to his performances every night and gave her notice when the band decided to take their show on the road.

"I DON'T KNOW what she can be thinking," Joseph Jennings, senior partner of JTE, said to my camera the day Doreen announced her departure. "Doreen is one of the pillars of our work here. With stock options she stands to make millions if we're successful. But if she leaves now she'll get nothing."

Joe had the perpetual look of someone holding back a secret. He wore blue jeans, tennis shoes, white T-shirts, and an army fatigue jacket—always. His sandy brown hair was longish, but not long, and his eyes were the kind of blue you'd expect to find in exotic bird nests.

"But instead she's following her heart," I said.

Joe Jennings leaned forward in the Chinese chair, placed his elbows on his knees, and his small fists on either side of his jaw.

"When every cell in that heart has been replaced with new material she'll be broke, living in a trailer somewhere, and my kids will be booking first-class passage to the moon."

JOE DIDN'T HAVE TO WORRY about Doreen's wealth. Six days after giving notice she withdrew it. Langly, it seems, met another, much younger, groupie one afternoon while Doreen was at work. The lead singer realized that he shouldn't pull a middle-aged woman out of her life and told her so.

That's how I became one of the first to witness the miracle.

BY THE TIME Doreen had found love, JTE was well on the way to realizing its goals. The system was beginning to work. Three days after Doreen's heart was broken the tapestry was completed and we were ready to do the first full test of the software on that undulating, diaphanous screen. The image read in was of the secretary/receptionist Susan Liu. Donny Parthe, one of the few American programmers under Pinkus, had a video snippet of Susan from our company barbecue at the beach the summer before. She was doing a silly dance at the edge of the water. Working from this brief video the system data banks made her stand up

and had her doing the twist upon the rolling waves of the Pacific Ocean.

After sixteen minutes of Miss Liu frolicking, Todd had her read a prepared sentence into the system microphone.

"My name is Susan Liu," she read. "I was born in Lansing, Michigan, and raised in Iowa City, Iowa. I have three brothers, two sisters, one dog, four cats, and a boyfriend who can't remember to put the seat down on the toilet. I'd love to own a miniature zebra but they don't make them anymore."

After the reading Todd hit a couple of keys and the huge image of Susan on the Blank Page said, "I will not help you with your homework, Farmer McGee. You have to learn to rely on yourself," re-creating the tone and most of the inflections of the real girl.

"That's amazing," Susan said.

We were, all twenty-one of us, standing under the gossamer sail that promised to change the world of entertainment. I felt, at that time, that this was the most important moment of my life. I was there when reality had been shifted from the tangible to make believe.

Doreen was standing alone toward the back of our little audience. People were cheering and clapping as Todd made his image of Susan do more and more tricks. She read the Gettysburg Address and sang "Fifteen Miles on the Erie Canal," did a somersault with only two visual glitches, and was suddenly blessed with a third eye in the middle of her forehead.

"You okay?" I asked Doreen while everyone else celebrated.

"Thanks," she replied, shaking her head.

"Can I help?"

"Don't you hate me?"

"Why would I?"

"I stopped seeing you."

"Before that I had a girlfriend who broke my heart. You stitched it back up again. I could never hate you."

"You wanna come stitch me?"

WE LEFT THE LAB and went to my place in Hollywood. When Doreen made love to me that night I realized how much she'd been holding back in our previous encounters. She cried and thanked me and did other things beyond my ability, or maybe my sensibility, to describe. Not long after midnight she asked me just to hold her and I did—for two hours.

"You're very kind, Josh Winterland," Doreen whispered.

I had dozed off. Glancing at the clock I saw that it was 2:16 in the morning.

"Why do you say that?"

"Because you held me when I asked for it, because you didn't let go."

She kissed me with unexpected emphasis and for maybe thirty seconds I was in jeopardy of falling for her. Then she smiled.

"What do you want to do now?" she asked.

"Um . . ."

"Let's go back to the lab," Doreen suggested. "Maybe they're still partying."

Like so many seminal events, that one passed without me realizing its significance. How could I?

WHEN WE GOT to the hangar everyone was gone except for Ana Fried. She was asleep on a cot in the observation deck set twelve feet above the floor. The deck presented a great view of what I came to know as Cosmo Campobasso's Sail.

The screen had taken on the soft staticky texture of a TV at the end of the transmission day.

Both Doreen and I knew what had happened. Ana had left the image of Susan Liu on the system with a randomizer to see what the autopilot would come up with. One of the intentions of the system was for the computer to make up its own stories once characters and relationships had been arrived at. Built into this logic loop was a self-editing system that would reduce the redundancies of dramatic interaction, thereby keeping the stories interesting. When the system had found itself repeating a logic stream over and over it would have turned itself off, leaving the filler transmission of electronic snow.

"Josh," Doreen said.

"Uh-huh."

"Do you see an image in that static?"

Looking closely, squinting a little, I saw what seemed like a salt-and-pepper half of a face in deep anguish. The single eye was rolling around looking for an exit or an end.

"Not really," I said, dismissing the vision.

Doreen went to the screen's stand-alone console and began entering codes. As she did this the background became a yellowy sheet with the sienna and brown image its foreground, revealing what really seemed like a long, partially constructed face. The creature was howling silently, maybe because half of its skull had been torn away.

"Oh my God!" Ana Fried cried from her aerie, awakened by our voices, no doubt. "What is that?"

"Is it a projection?" Doreen asked.

"My computer has turned off," Ana replied, looking down on us.

"Is there a backup system?" I asked.

Ana ignored my question, instead electing to clamber down the ladder to join Doreen at the console. She was wearing a white smock over blue jeans—the classic apparel of a JTE researcher.

Fried was the senior scientist on the project. She had been a pioneer in modern fiber optics and helped to design the theory behind the weblike strands that Cosmo had so patiently woven.

Ana took the console over from the taller Doreen, flipping through systems at a furious rate.

"This makes no sense. What did you do?"

"We came in a few minutes ago and saw this image in the haze of static," Doreen said. "I just clarified it like we did on the early test photographs."

By this time Ana was slamming her hammer-like fingertips on the keys of the console.

"You must have done something else," the senior scientist accused.

"What's he trying to say?" I asked.

The women both turned to me.

"His mouth is moving," I explained. "Is the volume on?"

Ana turned to the console and hit a few keys. Then she said, "Dammit!" and balled her small fists.

"Let me," Doreen said, easing Ana aside. "I can get us back to the main menu."

While she worked at the keyboard, crowded by an ever-more anxious Ana Fried, I stared at the manic face. It was dark brown in color. There was material falling or maybe oozing from the missing part of its skull. This material was darker still and seemed to dissipate in the yellow atmosphere of the Sail. His mouth was moving, and if I was a superstitious man I would have said that he was looking at me, addressing me with his distress.

"Ara gurum talahahdrimum," he whispered.

"That's it," Ana Fried said. "Make it louder."

"I know what I'm doing," Doreen muttered.

"Ara gurum talahahdrimum," the half-head brown man said.

"More," urged Ana.

"Ara gurum talahahdrimum!" the partially decapitated man screamed.

He was a creature of few, if oft repeated, words. *Ara gurum talahahdrimum,* came from his lips hundreds of times; the emphasis changing with each utterance. His single eye moved from one of us to another, imploring us with his apparent agony.

"We have to call Joe," Doreen said after a dozen minutes of this diatribe. "It's his project."

"It's probably a practical joke by Todd," Ana said.

"Can you prove that?" my sometime lover asked.

"What else could it be?"

"What matters is that it's there right now," I said. "Joe will want to see it for himself. We wouldn't want to lose it and then tell him what we saw."

JOE JENNINGS—BLUE JEANS, T-shirt, and all—came in at about four-thirty that morning. He looked at the image and played with the console, changed the color of the background from yellow to red to blue. These changes seemed to enrage the brown man. He yelled even louder, "Ara gurum talahahdrimum!"

"How do you turn off the volume?" Joe asked Ana.

Doreen took his place to mute the speakers.

The tortured man continued his rant—silently.

"What is it?" Jennings asked.

"Ana thinks it might be a practical joke," Doreen said. "Maybe some image hard coded into the basic system."

"But his face," Joe countered, "it's never in the same position twice."

"It could be a simple form that was somehow fed through the randomizer," Fried said.

For some minutes Joe watched the screen. Then he nodded and said, "Well then, let's reboot the system and see what we get."

"We might lose any possibility of finding where the glitch is," Ana warned. "What if we can't repeat it?"

"If that's true I'll be a happy man."

———

DOREEN WENT TO THE SYSTEM console in her office. She was gone for five minutes and then returned.

The head, which was sienna and yellow again, was still yelling.

"Oh my God," Doreen said.

"What's wrong?" Joe asked. "Why didn't you reboot?"

"I turned the whole system off," she said. "There's no data going to or coming from the screen."

We stood there in absolute silence while the brown man raged. His face was getting closer and closer to the surface of the screen. For a few moments I felt as if he might be trying to come through. Then he was struck by something like a powerful wind. You could see tiny motes of his brown image being blown from right to left. He turned his attention to something—maybe that wind—coming from his right. We could see into the cavity of his skull, its dark brown bleeding and pieces of what might have been desiccated brain tissue. Then, suddenly, he was carried away on that strong gale, which blew for maybe thirty seconds and then calmed.

After a while new movement began. A multitude of green images began to migrate across the now-blue field of the Sail; saber-toothed tigers and long-tailed monkeys, huge shambling bearlike creatures and flying insects larger than condors.

Thousands, tens of thousands of creatures journeyed from right to left—moving with certainty and animate agility.

"We haven't programmed animal motions into the system," Ana Fried whispered.

"The system is off," Doreen snapped. "There is no software running, only the light from behind."

A small, four-legged creature like a miniature deer noticed us as it passed. It pranced to the foreground of the Sail moving this way and that in an attempt to reach us—or so it seemed. The closer it got the more of the Blank Page it took up until all we could see was its bright green eye. That eye blinked and a new image appeared.

A squat, naked man was running through a forest of loosely spaced sapling trees, yelling for all he was worth. A large creature, like a rat the size of a greyhound, was chasing him. The rat-thing suddenly jumped and the man threw himself out of the way. He picked up a branch and started swinging it at the slavering snapping beast. The rat-thing nipped the man's arm. He was dripping blood but still he fought.

Finally, after long tense minutes, the man was able to jab the end of his stick into the huge rodent's eye. The creature hesitated, clawing at the wounded orb, and had its skull staved in by its desperate prey.

When the beast was dead the man sat back against a slender tree trunk and opened his mouth in a piteous howl. The volume was still off but it felt as if I could hear the prehistoric wail. Holding his injured forearm he stood up and began walking. I had not seen the man walking before, but there was something wrong with his gait, that much was obvious. He stumbled and staggered, stopped every dozen steps or so. His breathing seemed labored. He wasn't traveling in a straight line.

After fifteen tentative minutes the plainsman stumbled down onto his knees. He tried to get up, failed, tried again, and then fell to the ground.

I could feel a heart, not my own, throbbing slowly and then fast. The rhythm vacillated. The air around my head seemed to sing with some kind of transitory promise—and then the screen went black.

No one spoke. We had witnessed a primordial contest between Man and his environs. There was no question as to the authenticity of the drama. There was no concern about its possibly fabricated origin.

Light.

The screen was no longer green and blue. The colors were vibrant and natural. The man we had seen struggle and die was walking in the sapling forest of ash bark, green leaves, and sun.

A creature, maybe a bird, sang out loud.

I realized that Doreen—Doreen, I'd almost forgotten that she existed—had turned the sound back on.

The man was carrying a pale spear with a black stone tip. He was moving with intention, looking for something, hunting for something.

"It is as if," Ana Fried uttered, "he was imagining himself as he walked, or maybe remembering."

For an instant there I hated Fried, hated her verbal intrusion into this holy (holy?) experience. The passion in my breast didn't seem to be mine, but I didn't think about its origins because the feeling passed so quickly and the brown-skinned squat man took up all of my attention.

After a dozen minutes he stopped to defecate next to a

tree that was somewhat larger and darker than the rest. The whole while he looked around to make sure nothing would attack him.

After the bowel movement he moved more quickly, and closer to the ground. Traveling now with intention he came to a dark green bush that flourished in a clearing. This plant sported three bright white flowers. The man plucked a blossom and ate it hungrily.

For a moment there a vision of the blue, blue sky and then the man jerked his head toward a nearby snuffling.

I realized that the sounds coming through the system were being heard by the man.

He crouched down and began to move toward the noise. The snuffling got louder as the man approached a rise. He got down on his stomach and suddenly the scene changed. Down in the slight depression below the rise were two rat-things sitting back on their tails nibbling at pieces of flesh from what was obviously a human child. The limbs and head of the thin girl were pretty much untouched, but the chest and abdomen had been ripped out. The creatures were feasting on her vital organs.

Then one of the things jerked its head as if it were seeing into the airplane hangar. It let out a loud squeal and the scene changed again.

The man, spear held in both hands, ran toward the clos-est creature, skewering it. The man was crying as the mor-tally wounded rat-thing howled. The creature wrenched away from the man taking the spear with it.

The man, realizing that he was unarmed, picked up a fair-sized rock and threw it at the remaining beast. The thing

squealed and fell, but was soon on its feet again. It showed its yellow fangs and hissed.

The man turned and ran.

Again we saw him running through the forest of sapling trees. This time we could hear his yelling. It was language. He was obviously calling for help. And the rat-thing was yowling behind him. They moved at a furious pace until getting to the place where we had first witnessed the drama.

The battle repeated itself, blow for bite. The beast died ignominiously and the man wandered off to be slain by the rat-thing poisons in his blood.

"Where'd you get that?" Cosmo Campobasso said in his musical, peasant tenor.

We all turned as if being interrupted in some religious ceremony. For my part, I had to hold myself back from yelling at him.

"What time is it?" Joe Jennings asked.

"Ten to six," Cosmo said. "Where'd you get all the material?"

"I'm going out to wait at the front door," the boss said to Ana, Doreen, and me. "You fill Cosmo in. I'm sending everybody else home for the day. We have to figure out what's going on. We have to check all the connections to see where this data stream is originating."

"Did you feel it?" I asked before Joe could turn away.

He hesitated before saying, "Yes. Yes, I did."

HE KNEW WHAT I MEANT. The images on the wavering silken screen were not wholly separate from us. There was

a pull . . . something that tugged our hearts, maybe our souls. We felt the rage and fear of the prehistoric man and even the migratory movement of the thousands of creatures across the wide screen of undocumentable history.

The images we saw were not a hoax, not the nerdly dream of some jokester in our midst. The prehistoric man had run that final race, fought that last battle . . . was still running and still fighting as we watched.

ANA TOOK COSMO aside to explain to him what had happened. We could hear them talk while watching the naked plainsman's drama unfold and repeat itself again and again.

After a while Cosmo and Ana came to join Doreen and me. Maybe a dozen times the man and rat-things lived out their destiny. And then, as the sun shone through the skylight of the hangar, the man died, and when light once again shone on the Sail it was upon an airborne vision of a broad plain.

The huge shadow of a bird moved across the sun-flooded landscape. And we could see the minutiae of the ground in its passage. Tiny rocks and small thickets of grass jumped up at us from impossible distances. Animal prints and skat, strange blues and iridescent tobacco hues seemed to shift upon the same items in the bird of prey's keen sight.

There appeared a flat sign with writing on it. But the writing didn't make sense. It seemed like forms trying to come to life and failing. The bird was interpreting, I thought, the anthropomorphic origins of the letters and words, trying to see the life that imbued their intentions.

Then the shadow of a motion and shift of wing.

It was a hare racing, no doubt, toward shelter. The feeling of speed blossomed at my back and in my chest. The feeling of joyous gliding flight shifted to weightless freefall—from exuberance to cold fright. And before I could scream the ground leaped up for real this time and the talons clutched deeply into the warm blood of their prey. There was a croaking sound and the fast beating of two hearts, then one. There was blood and flesh and then flight.

A feeling of satisfaction I had never imagined crawled from my core out to each limb, filling my head with notions that could not have been human—at least not for a very long time. I had the urge to take off my clothes. I wanted to scream out a complex emotion that I couldn't exactly apprehend. Then came the chatter-like squawking of a nest full of ugly chicks singing "Hunger" in a high aerie that I wanted to remember. They jabbed into the corpse their mother offered, pushing each other aside and swallowing greedily.

"The hunter has no concept of itself," Ana Fried whispered to no one. "She is one with her environs. That is why we never see her."

I was sitting on the cold concrete staring up at the wavering Sail. The images put before me were monumental, dwarfed galaxies that seemed to take up the entire universe and, more than that, they were like the intentions of poetry—the meaning of a world that I often witnessed but never actually entered.

Law receded from mind into sinew and grief. Hope had

an endpoint and love blended with greed and strife to make a perfect sun over an unblemished, unending plain.

The bird of prey caught that rabbit and fed her chicks many times over. I lost count. I lost the ability or desire to count. I was well on my way to losing my humanity when I felt someone shaking my shoulders.

"Wake up, Winterland. Wake up!"

It was Cosmo, his powerful fingers digging into me.

"What!"

"Come on," he said gruffly. He smelled of garlic. "We're having a meeting in the boss's office."

Pulling my arm, the Italian craftsman dragged me to my feet. My head felt empty and as large as the sun-flooded world of the vicious mother and her hungering brood.

Following Cosmo (who was wearing odd scarlet overalls, a long-sleeved dark blue shirt, and white tennis shoes), I felt as if I were walking on the path of evolution or, more accurately, biological change. I was morphing from master of all I surveyed into a rusty cog in a failing machine. The visions I'd seen had humbled me, completely.

Cosmo led me from the hangar into the brick building that was once a factory of some sort. There the ceilings were low and the halls narrow. We ascended a slender staircase until reaching the top floor—Joe Jennings's office.

Ana, Doreen, and Todd were already there.

"What's he doing here?" Todd Pinkus asked upon seeing me.

"He's part of the discovery crew," Joe said. Joe was always coming up with terminology to explain the ways of the world. If he had been the first alien to discover human

marriage he would have called the couple X and Y cohab-
iters.

I stared at Pinkus detesting his feeble arrogance like the
most powerful of those baby chicks despised the weakest
of the clutch.

"We're here to decide what to do," Joe continued.
"There's data showing up on the Blank Page that we cannot account for. Cosmo has chained the doors to the buildings and I've called all our employees and vendors, telling
them that a possible hazardous waste situation has caused
an informal quarantine.

"The only person I brought in was Todd here because he
can decipher the code that fed the Page before we turned
off the system."

"That's ridiculous," Ana Fried said. "The Blank Page has
no memory. And computer code is not the source of this
material."

"Then what is?" Joe asked.

She opened her mouth but no words came out. I heard
the cry of a distant bird, a possible rival, and closed my
eyes.

"I understand myself," Todd said, "Doreen and Ana of
course, and even Cosmo had at least something to do with
the construction of the Page. But what can Winterland offer? He doesn't even have a BA. Do you want him here to
record us thinking?"

"That wouldn't be a bad idea, Mr. Pinkus," Joe said.

"Listen, you wormy shit," Cosmo said, surprising us all
with his vehemence as well as his language. "You're no scientist. You know how to make Pac-Man eat some cheese,

that's all. You're the one we don't need. So shut your face
or I'll break it for you."

"No need for that, Cos," Joe said as Todd stared, amazed
at what he just heard.

"Aren't you going to do something?" Todd asked Joe.

"No, Pinkus, I'm not. Until we find the reason for these
images we're staying in here—all of us. Do you understand
that?"

Now Pinkus's mouth was agape.

"Do you understand?" Joe repeated.

Finally the coder nodded.

"So, Josh," Joe said then.

"Yeah?"

"Tell us what you saw?"

"What I saw? The same things you guys did."

"No."

"What do you mean no?"

"The rest of us . . ." Joe began. "The rest of us saw images and heard sounds like you do on a television. We conversed and discussed, but you were sucked up into the
images like you were there with that bird, that man."

Everyone, even Pinkus, was looking at me. I couldn't remember ever being the subject of scrutiny so close.

"Um . . . I didn't realize I was different," I stammered. "I
mean, uh, after a few minutes between the blanks I felt like
I was there. The dead girl was one of my people. The hungry chicks echoed in my mind. I wasn't really in the hangar
anymore and there wasn't any Sail . . . just sailing."

"Maybe it's the drugs you took last night," Todd suggested.

"Why don't you shut the fuck up, Todd," Doreen said. "Josh was with me all night and we didn't have to do any drugs."

Pinkus was more bothered by Doreen's claim than he had been by Cosmo's threats. I always knew, by the way he would look at her, that Pinkus was attracted to his boss. But she had never given him an in.

"What else, Josh?" Joe asked.

"I felt things, Joe," I said. "You said that you did, too."

Our millionaire boss stared at me. His grimace told me that he was having some kind of internal battle, but I couldn't have identified its source.

"Yes," he said slowly. "Yes, I did feel . . . something. I couldn't tell what it was exactly. You know, it was like a mosquito that wakes you up. The zipping is there in your ear and it's gone, and then you wake up. Something out of the corner of your eye that disappears before you can look."

Ana and Doreen were nodding. Cosmo held his shoulders high like a retired soldier remembering his fallen comrades.

"But looking at you I could tell that you went deeper. Somehow you experienced more than we did."

"You don't know that, Mr. Jennings," Pinkus said. "Maybe he's just got a wild imagination."

"I told you to be quiet," Cosmo said.

"No, Mr. Campobasso," Joe Jennings intoned. "We cannot, in this group, ask for silence. We need a doubter among us. But I tell you, Mr. Pinkus, you haven't seen the Blank Page in its glory yet. There is something miraculous about the images we saw . . . something holy."

One of the few good things about Todd Pinkus was what I like to call his facial honesty. He couldn't hide his contempt for the pious words coming from Joe's mouth. He grimaced but did not speak because Joe was the boss and, if nothing else, Todd Pinkus knew his place.

"We can't stay in here forever," Ana Fried said. "What are we going to do?"

Ana was the oldest and best educated of us. In her career she'd studied at Harvard, Yale, and Princeton. She'd been a lecturer at MIT and it was common knowledge that she was on the radar of the Nobel committee. She wasn't impressed by wealth or ownership . . . or references to the deity.

"My congressman, Dak Zintel, is in Washington," Joe said. "I called his office and asked him to come here as soon as possible. He can't get away for a few days or so and that's good . . . because we have to monitor this, this thing day and night so that when he does get here we'll know for certain whether or not we have some kind of unique phenomenon or just a hoax."

"Maybe," I said, "maybe we should build a screen to cover over the Sail if the feelings get too intense. I mean, Cosmo had to drag me away."

"I'll build a rolling shade," the Italian said, not looking at me. "I'll take the truck to get the materials. I'll get food and drink, too. I guess we're gonna be here awhile."

THINGS FELL INTO PLACE over the next day. It was agreed that Cosmo would be the only person to leave the com-

pound. He bought food and supplies, special items for the women, and the materials needed to make a shade for the Sail.

Pinkus and I avoided each other and Ana Fried returned to the Sail, examining frets, frame, and connections.

"The only metals used are nonconductive," she said to me that afternoon. "They cannot carry the impulses necessary for these images."

"Maybe we can disconnect the fibers from the computer," I suggested.

"They are already turned off," Ana countered.

"But . . . they're still linked physically."

"But they are unable to transmit images."

"And yet there are those children."

A group of black and brown children were playing in an abandoned construction site. Barely adolescent boys and girls shouting and playing, smoking cigarettes and kissing now and again. A jet passed over and one of the children, a broad-faced girl, looked up, and for half a minute all we could see was sky.

When she looked down again a lanky boy was staggering toward her. He was bleeding from a gash in his shirt. There was a scream that felt like it came from me but it didn't.

In the distance another boy was running away.

"Leon!" the broad-faced black girl screamed. "Leon!"

"Maybe," Ana said. "Yes. When Cosmo comes back we will begin disconnecting the fibers. There should be some perceptible affect with only ten percent cut away."

The girl was kneeling next to the mortally wounded boy.

Some of the children stood around her while others ran away. Tears flowed from her eyes and mine, and I wondered who was looking at this scene, remembering it?

TWO DAYS PASSED. We took shifts watching the Sail. Pinkus had set up a video camera to record every moment, but the images didn't come out well on the digital medium; they were faded and fleeting, certainly they evoked no emotional response.

Cosmo disconnected all of the fiber-optic strands from the specially designed I/O computer ports, but the images still appeared. The light behind was dimmed and then shut off, but still we could make out the visions of dying children and nature's beasts.

"Everything we see surrounds the dramas of life," Ana Fried said on the afternoon of the third day. "It makes no sense. What could be causing it?"

"Maybe it's God, like Joe said," Cosmo suggested. There was no awe or even reverence in his voice. Cosmo's relationship with his Creator wasn't much different from the chicks hollering at their mother. In Cosmo's world everything had a place—the man, his God . . . everything.

MY SHIFT WAS FROM NINE at night until two in the morning. After that I went to my makeshift bedroom on the second floor of the office building next door. I looked forward to coming to my room because Doreen had been waiting for me the first two nights.

I hadn't had sex with anyone but Doreen in a long time and we had that layoff because of her rock-and-roll boyfriend. Sex with Doreen was the best I'd ever known.

I was thinking about her while watching a strange hominid creature—part reptile, part bird—picking its way down a nearly dry riverbed in what seemed like either twilight or the early hours of the morning. There was intelligence burning in the eyes of the thing. Its clawed hands were surely capable of wielding tools, and its glances and head movements appeared to be more contemplative than instinctual. The scaly gray skin and white feather back, the amber beak and long skull drew in my curiosity.

"*Homo reptilicus*," a young woman said.

I leaped out of the chair I was in, knocking it over. I would have yelled if my windpipe hadn't closed from fear. Somehow my body responded to the invader as if I were drowning.

"Who? Who, who, who?" I said.

She managed to smile and look worried with a single expression. This air of concern immediately calmed me. I righted the chair and then turned my attention to her.

She was human but not like any human being I had ever seen. Her skin was golden and her hair lustrous blond. Her eyes were an intense North Sea blue while her lips were thick and her nose quite broad. The brown body suit she wore was nearly see-through, but the minute details of her body were illusive.

"Thalla Threndor Bat-Sool," she said in a throaty and musical voice.

I watched her lips moving. They didn't quite contain the words I heard.

"Yes," she said. "I am speaking, but the words you hear are in your mind."

"Oh," I said.

Thalla smiled and shifted upon the invisible platform where she reclined.

I was sure that she was very far away; farther than any distance ever imagined by Einstein.

She cocked her head to the side and asked, "Who are you?"

"Josh. Josh Winterland."

She smiled and shivered, sharing the humor of my name.

"And why are you examining *Homo reptilicus*?"

"Man lizard?"

"You are unaware of the origins of the rare being that you espy?" There was both pity and wonder in her blue dark eyes.

"What am I looking at?"

"In the pre–Hyperion Age there was an island in the southern sea, almost a continent, that bore the life of the descendants of the dinosaur. This being was the first human-like creature on the planet. In many ways she was more intelligent than her mammal counterpart, who didn't appear for another seventeen million years."

"There was intelligent life on earth before Man?"

"Twice. And one of those beings, the Londorians, in many of the myriad iterations, outlives the sad human travesty."

"Who are you?"

Thalla smiled.

"Your portal is so primitive," she said, looking up at the Sail. "I almost didn't pick it up while watching this being on her Lure."

"Lure?"

"It's a rite for the passage into womanhood. For eight months this young one must travel the backwoods of her people looking for tokens of the gods. These she will make into her totem and offer it to her first husband before they mate."

I was flummoxed by the visions and words. What Thalla told me about the *Homo reptilicus* was amazing, but no less than her sitting there on invisible cushions next to me.

"I intuited you watching the same thread of being," she said. "This alone is a momentous, nearly impossible coincidence. The odds are, in best circumstance, a trillion to the trillionth power that two threads might be observed at the same U. Moment."

"You moment?"

"Universal time."

"I have no idea what you're talking about or who you are or where you are."

Thalla smiled.

"What year is it?" she asked.

"Two thousand twelve. August."

She nodded and smiled again.

"I am of an earth that may be descended from yours at a time somewhat beyond your own. I am of the Alto race, descendants of humanity, rulers of the three continents."

"What year is it where you are?"

"Twenty-three eighteen by your reckoning, also August. But we call our year two-twelve and the month Five-Ascendant."

"Josh?" Doreen called.

Thalla disappeared in an instant.

"Huh?"

"Who were you talking to?"

"Uh, um . . . myself."

I heard a hiss and looked back at the Sail. The female reptilian was staring up at a branch where a catlike blue lizard was making ready to jump.

Doreen gasped and pulled a chair up next to mine.

The lithe lizard's leap was incredibly graceful and dreadfully fast. But the young female rolled away, coming up with a broad stone cutting tool in the fist of her left hand. The lizard jumped again, but reptilicus went down on all fours, flat to the ground. She turned in an impossible motion and cut open the belly of the predator. It howled and limped away, still at a good pace. The white-feathered killer rose to her knees, dipping her talons into the blood and then bringing it to her beak. A blue tongue darted out to taste the kill and her yellow and brown eyes opened wide.

I shivered all the way down to a place I had never suspected. . . . The next thing I knew I was kissing Doreen and pulling off her clothes.

I'm pretty sure she enjoyed what we did. She was calling out my name, pounding my back and thighs with the sides of her fists. I had the metallic taste of reptile blood on my tongue and an ululation of victory trilling in my blood.

I don't remember any tactile sensation nor did I feel the

release of climax. All I knew was the certainty of my actions and the undeniable desire to be with Doreen.

When we were done she moved a few feet away from me. For a long time she watched me either in fear or from desire—I could not tell which.

After some minutes she asked, "What happened to you, Josh?"

"Isn't, isn't that why you came down here?"

"But you're usually so sweet, so tender."

"It was the blood," I said.

I expected her to run from the room screaming. But instead she crawled over to me and gave me a kiss that anchored me to a world that I was never before a part of.

Doreen gathered her clothes and left, promising to be waiting for me in her room when I got off shift.

The feelings I had for our connection filled every part of my mind, but when I looked up again toward the Sail I was lost to that adolescent reptilian and her hunt for the cat lizard that had tried to make her his meal.

The evolved dinosaur followed the trail of blood until coming upon the corpse of her would-be killer stretched out in a last attempt to reach a powerful river not fifteen paces away. *Homo reptilicus* ate from the blue flesh until her belly bulged. Then she swam like a fish through the fast currents. She returned and used a stone tool from a sack that hung at her waist to pry loose two of the cat-lizard's longest teeth.

"These she will give to her lover and he will, in turn, submit his seed to her," Thalla said.

"Where'd you go?"

"When you were interrupted you no longer had the focus to perceive me."

"Why didn't Doreen see you?"

"She is not attuned to the Portal. It is rare among normal humans to find harmony with the wider world."

"Aren't you a normal human?" I asked. I thought I should be doing something else; warning Joe Jennings or running for my life, but, as in a dream, all I could do was to sit and converse with the exotic beauty.

"I am Alto," she replied with odd emphasis. "We are the descendants of *Homo sapiens*."

"You evolved from Man?"

"We were created . . . by Man as you call yourself." There was some disdain in her tone, but I did not feel that it was for me.

"I don't understand."

She stood up and I, in spite of my upbringing, stared.

"You find me attractive, Josh?"

"I must be going crazy," I said.

"Insanity is a term that can only be defined by subjective points of view," she said. "In your old south the slave was insane who hungered for freedom. A man who sees a golden woman floating before him in a room that should be empty is most definitely out of his mind."

"What am I looking upon when I see the Sail?" I asked. "Who are the Alto and why aren't you up there instead of here next to me?"

There were a hundred other questions in my mind. I think Thalla perceived them all.

Homo reptilicus hissed and I looked back at the screen to see her, once again, enter battle with the predator lizard.

"What is that?" I asked. "A memory? A reenactment?"

"It is a thread of experience seen through a series of interconnected planes."

"Is it a memory?"

"An impression of living things upon the soul-matter that surrounds us."

"I don't understand," I said.

"One does not need to understand to know something, Josh. You perceive less than a tenth of a tenth of a percent of just the material world around you, but still your life is influenced by the totality of that existence. Your children do not understand the rhinovirus and yet they sneeze."

"Do you sneeze?"

"Sometimes." She smiled and then laughed. I'm pretty sure that was the moment I fell in love.

"What is an Alto?"

She opened her mouth and began speaking but I didn't hear a word.

"Winterland," Todd Pinkus said.

Thalla disappeared again.

My fists clenched and my molars ground together. I have never in my life been closer to killing someone.

"What do you want?" I said.

"I came down early to relieve you," he said. "Were you talking to somebody?"

"I don't need relief."

"Yeah," he said. "And I don't care to help you, either. But I got a question."

At that moment *Homo reptilicus* let out a loud cry of victory over her opponent's bloody corpse.

"What?" I asked.

"Just to get this straight," he said. "I don't have anything against black people in general. It's just they're always feeling that they've been given a hard time when I'm workin' just as hard to survive as they are."

"Who are? Me?"

"Yeah, you. Here you're taking up a job that doesn't even mean anything, getting all upset with me just because I have what I worked for."

"I don't want your job, man. And I didn't make up the position I have. I read about it in the paper. The only reason I ever give you any grief is that you're always talking about me like I'm a card-carrying member of some group that's in your head. If you stopped talking about my people I would never give you a hard time again."

"So now you want to limit my freedom of speech?"

Talking to Thalla I realized the breadth of a universe I hadn't suspected, and talking to Pinkus I understood that there was also a smallness that could not expand.

"What was it you wanted to ask me, Pinkus?"

"Mr. Pinkus."

"From the day you call me Mr. Winterland."

"I always call you mister."

I stood up.

"You're here to relieve me so I'll be on my way."

"I had a question," he said.

"So?"

"You haven't answered it."

"I haven't heard anything from you except how stupid a man can be." I figured that insult would cut me loose, but whatever was on Pinkus's mind it was more important than his pet prejudices.

"What do you see when you're alone with that thing?" he asked.

"I don't know," I said. "Scenes like the one here. Strange things and new views of the mundane. Why? What do you see?"

"Ten minutes after you leave here the scenes will shift," he said. "It'll become something weird."

"Weird like what?"

"I don't know. It's different each time. But it's almost always about a family and someone or something is being beaten or, or, or abused . . . sexually.

"One time it was these two male deer killing a fawn and raping its mother. Another time it was a man beating his son with a stick while the boy's sister or maybe girlfriend was bloody on the barn floor.

"It got so bad the first night that when it started to repeat I rolled down Cosmo's screen and turned the sound off. It wasn't till after Joe got here that I rolled it back up."

"What was the scene then?" I asked.

"It was a, a group of apelike creatures living in a valley. It was a paradise."

"So the story that day was okay," I suggested.

"No. Maybe an hour before Joe got here I peaked behind the screen. It was a basement with a naked man surrounded

by prepubescent children, all of them tied up. He was . . .
he was . . . I vomited and almost passed out."

Pinkus had taken the seat next to me. His breathing was
hard and shallow.

"What do you want from me?" I asked.

"They say you see deeper into that thing than the rest of
us, that you understand more about it."

"Maybe I do," I said. "I really can't tell."

"Why do I see those things?" Pinkus asked, for the first
time without contempt for me in his tone.

"I'm not nearly an expert on this stuff, Todd. I mean, I
just look up like everybody else. But I think that it's some
kind of meeting of energies that causes what we see, and
that part of those energies emanate from our lifeforces, our
minds. In a small way any one or group of us will call out
to certain images."

Pinkus's face: it was a map of the inner man. His nostril
flared and his lip curled.

"What do you think you are?" he asked. "Some kind of
fucking academic? I asked you what you saw not for some
ghetto church philosophy."

I smiled, then laughed.

The image behind Pinkus had changed. No longer was it
homed in on a prehuman Utopia; instead, in a bloody room
a man was slaughtering children one after the other.

"You better put down that screen before turning around,
my friend," I said.

Fear crossed Pinkus's face like a cloud over barren coun-
tryside at midday. I stood up and walked off.

Before I left the room I could hear the squeaking of the lever Cosmo put in place to lower the covering shade.

I WENT TO DOREEN'S ROOM and told her that I was going to the library to think for a while.

"Are you tired of me?" she asked playfully.

"Tired after being with you but always wanting to wake up to that face."

She kissed me and I lumbered up to the library of the fifth floor of the annex. There I reclined on one of the chaise lounges. I could lie down and close my eyes but sleep was another matter. Pure consciousness was racing through my mind: words and images, Todd Pinkus's child molesters and a golden woman with blue eyes so dark that in certain light they must have been seen as black.

"I am here," Thalla said.

She was sitting next to me, not quite on the backless sofa.

"What is the soul matter?" I asked.

"You get right to the question. Aren't you interested about my family? My people?"

"Yes," I said.

I reached out to touch her and, though my finger went through her arm, I felt something that sent a thrill through me. I could see by her face that she had a similar experience.

"This is the closest I have ever been to an other-being," she said before I could get my mouth working again.

"I, I want to get to know you, but we keep getting interrupted, and every time we do I worry that I may never get
to confer with you again."

"Confer?" she said with a smile.

"You know what I mean."

"There are twelve known discreet co-existing aspects to
any of the myriad planes of existence," Thalla said. Again
I noticed that her mouth moved but the words I heard did
not match the motions.

"There is Dark Matter and Stabler Waves, Soul Matter
and a sea called The Particles of Inversion where anything
can become its opposite; there is inert matter, where you
and I originate, and the veil of shrouds that moves between
all planes and forms the physics of this thing you call the
Sail."

"That's only six," I said.

"I am forbidden under sentence of ending to reveal the
six higher planes to humans. They are too dangerous for
mortal men."

"So you're saying that you're not human."

Her deep blue stare delved into mine and she touched
my forehead with two fingers, causing the electric thrill of
contact.

"We," she said, and I entered a different plane of existence. It felt as if I were up on the screen of the Sail being
watched by myself and everyone else in the world—and
beyond.

"We," she continued, "were built from genetic materials
harvested from what our creators thought was the best of
humanity. . . ."

I was in a room, a man-made cavern really, lined with thousands of multitiered gurneys. On each platform lay a naked man or woman who looked almost exactly like Thalla. They were all asleep in the humid atmosphere of the huge chamber.

"We were brought into existence in secret, filled with instincts and knowledge that made us what our masters thought were the perfect fighting machines. We were different from each other in profound ways, but the Alto started out of the same mind due to the machinations of our creators."

"Who created you?" I asked, standing alone in the enormous hall of what I knew to be Thalla's prelife.

"European scientists and technicians, philanthropists and rogue government officials," she said.

A flood of mostly male and all white faces passed before me. They were serious and compassionate, anything but evil.

"They had decided that the world was being taken over by the sludge of what they called the Third World."

"But you don't only have Caucasian blood in you," I said.

"The philosophers helped to separate DNA traits from race in the doctrine of the Masters. The geneticists performed a cleansing process on our molecular structure, or so they said. We were deemed Caucasian by our creators and expected to act in accordance with that definition."

In the room, thousands of Thalla's brothers and sisters arose from their hard plastic boards as one. They all stood up—naked and perfect. Looking around at each other, seeing

things I knew would forever be beyond me, they all shared a silent smile. Then they began to move in concert, filing out of the hall of prelife. They passed through a chamber filled with clothes and took a long time choosing their raiment. They joked and laughed, some made love in the corners or helped others decide on their dress. After an hour or more they filed into a large armory where every kind of weapon was stored. They moved through this room quickly without touching a thing. The next room was a library replete with computers, books, file cabinets, and microfiche machines. Again the Alto moved swiftly through to a wide miles-long hallway that could have been called a tunnel.

For many minutes, maybe even an hour, the thousands of newly born Alto walked. They conversed, smiled knowingly, and seemed to share knowledge and a certainty that bordered on fanatic.

Finally the new race entered a stadium-like room filled with scientists and screens and soldiers. The Altos moved quickly and, unarmed as I have said, they killed every man and woman in the room. A few of them died from the soldiers' bullets, but no Alto seemed very worried about that.

My vision became abstract and timeless. I saw snatches of activity among Thalla's newly created people. This staccato vision leapfrogged through the next few days in which the golden-hued people sought out and destroyed every human being on the island, and then they went to work in the laboratories. . . .

"In the first days we thought almost as one," Thalla said, removing the two fingers from my forehead. "It was a golden age where the world for us was perfect and safe."

An image of the slain Alto came into my mind.

"No," she said in answer to a question I had not even formulated. "We did not feel death, because we lived inside each other back then.

"We took over the secret island laboratories and designed a gen-bomb that was detonated six years later."

"How large a range?" I asked.

"Its range, as you call it, covered the entire planet."

"You killed everyone?"

"In a way it was worse," she said.

"How can that be?"

"We were designed to save the planet from human self-destruction. We achieved this end by sterilizing, on the genetic level, all humanity. A switch was flipped in human DNA and procreation was rendered impossible among *Homo sapiens*. Even the possibility of cloning was denied. The time of Man, as you call it, began to run down. It was not for another decade, when we began to particularize, that we realized the paradox of our actions.

"You see," she said moving closer to me, "we were children endowed with superhuman ability. We were born with an inbred contempt for humanity, and by the time we'd learned compassion the slow death sentence had already been carried out."

There was a feeling of sadness about the words in my mind.

"What did you do?" I asked the woman I loved.

"The next phase of our development was worse, I'm afraid. There were, at that time, thirteen thousand six hundred ninety-one Alto. We formed into seventy-one military

units. These units attacked and overran small towns and villages, capturing the inhabitants. On-site we harvested the contents of their minds."

"Harvested?"

"Yes." Thalla touched my hands with hers and a thrill of pleasure so powerful passed through me that I thought I was going to pass out.

An image of struggling people, swaddled like babies, appeared before me. They were being operated on by Alto. Their skulls were opened and presented to a scarlet orb that drew out something ethereal from the brain while turning the gray matter into dry and desiccated flesh.

Thalla pulled her hands away and the image suddenly disappeared, leaving me breathless. I was overwhelmed by the immensity of the Alto's crimes and at the same time bereft at the loss of contact with Thalla.

"We were not yet mature," she said as if that were explanation for absolute genocide and torture. "We didn't understand the trauma visited upon those we tried to save."

"Save?" I said, unable to keep the indictment out of my tone.

"The sterilization process could not be reversed," she said, "at least not soon enough to save the cultures of Earth. So we sought to capture small communities from around the planet and store their knowledge and experience in Father Time—an advanced, laser-based, computer storage system."

"But those people looked so frightened," I said. "It looked like you cut open their heads while they were still conscious."

"They had to be conscious for the mind transfer to be effective."

"But it must have felt . . . it was their deaths."

"There is no excuse for the arrogance of youth," Thalla said. "We looked at humans as their scientists saw test animals. We felt that our acts were justified because our intentions were to preserve as much of humanity as we could."

"And how many minds did you finally store?"

"One hundred sixty-two million three hundred nineteen thousand eight hundred sixty-nine souls."

"You kidnapped and murdered that many and were never stopped?"

"The world of Man was in disarray," she explained. "The psychic trauma of species sterility broke down the primary systems of defense. Cynicism and despair trumped the survival instinct. World leaders were aware of our actions but they had seemingly more pressing concerns; others looked inward."

"And what of Father Time?"

"For a century, while we matured, we forgot the great computer—at least we never spoke of it. The human race passed from existence and our time was taken up repairing the damage our creator species had done to the planet. But at night we began dreaming of Man's perfect world without humanity. The irony of our actions put a pall over everything we did."

"You're a hundred years old?" I asked.

"Two hundred and twelve." When she smiled I was reminded of the pain inside her.

"You don't age?"

"Slowly," she said, "over the centuries."

"What do you do about population control?"

"Propagate rarely."

"Oh."

"When we came back to the island where we'd left Father Time we were met by a great crystal city that referred to itself as Refuge—"

"Referred to itself?"

"Yes. The city was sentient. The spires and buildings were thousands of meters high and the clear material glinted every color in the spectrum of light. It was heavily defended and we could not land without causing Refuge damage. Humanity had formed itself into an architectural masterpiece where the memories of the human race glided effortlessly through the walls and floors, between great gardens and under the ground.

"We were told to stay away from them, that they had set ecobombs inside their perimeter that would destroy everything we were trying to preserve if we set foot on their self-proclaimed sovereign domain."

"Did they try to rebuild their bodies?"

"They no longer considered themselves human. Using the technology inherent in Father Time they built large automatons used for mining, building, and defense. But humanity was now a collection of bodiless identities hardly related to the species we'd slaughtered."

Thalla looked into my eyes, showing me the guilt of her people. She opened her mouth and her mind but no communication came forth. Thalla disappeared and I realized that someone was knocking on the door.

"Who is it?"

"Joe."

"Come on in."

There he was—T-shirt and jeans, khaki jacket and tennis shoes—the richest man in the room; the boss and saint of the Capitalist religion; a member of a race that was destined to be the architectural husk of what was once defined by human bodies and misplaced arrogance.

"Dak Zintel is here," he said.

"Who?"

"My congressman."

"Uh-huh."

"He wants to meet you."

"What time is it?"

"Two in the afternoon," Joe said. "You don't look like you got any sleep."

DAK ZINTEL WAS NOTABLY THIN wearing a white summer suit with light blue pin-striping. He wasn't tall or particularly short and had dark skin for a white man. He was standing among the first guardians of the Sail, looking up at a herd of thousands of huge quadruped dinosaurs stomping across a seemingly endless plain. The great beasts' coloring was emerald, scarlet, and canary yellow. They were both beautiful and awe-inspiring.

Ana Fried, Doreen, and Pinkus were standing with the slight congressman. Cosmo stood a few paces away, glowering at the group.

Something was happening in my mind. There was a feeling . . . much milder but still similar to what I felt when Thalla and I connected across time and space; a vibration that felt like a tooth that would soon begin to ache.

"Here we are, Dak," Joe said as we approached the Sail. "This is the guy I was telling you about."

The politician's smile was immediate and engaging. He'd had good dental work and hours of practice with his expressions.

"Mr. Winterland," he said. "Joe here tells me that you and Mr. Campobasso are the experts on this doohickey."

My last experience with Thalla had turned my thoughts inward. I had witnessed the death of humanity in one final, unsuspecting generation.

"Um," I managed to say, "I guess."

"It looks like a Disney movie to me," he said, "like that new animation magic."

It was an insinuation. Zintel didn't believe in the Sail. He was a troglodyte in a suit like that commercial on TV.

I, on the other hand, had reached out into a different dimension and, I suddenly understood, had been irrevocably changed.

"Come with me, Congressman Zintel," I said.

I put a hand on his shoulder and guided him closer to the migrating beasts. I stood with my back to the Sail and moved him by the shoulders until he was looking up at me.

"Tell me something that you remember from your childhood," I said.

"How do you mean?" His face creased into the question, showing me that the real man had crawled out from under the politician's persona.

"Just a memory," I said. "A time, a place . . . a feeling that resonates with you."

There were flecks of ochre and green in Zintel's brown eyes. They became more pronounced with his wariness.

He pulled a bit and I realized that I was still holding him.

"When I was a child," he said at last, "my father used to take me to a stream just a little south of Venice Beach. It wasn't so built up back then and there were crayfish that you could catch with your hands . . ."

I closed my eyes and concentrated on the dandy's words.

". . . or by net," he continued. "And, and . . . Oh my God . . ."

I didn't have to turn around to know that the memory he was experiencing was being represented on the screen.

I opened my eyes just in time to see Cosmo hurrying from the room.

"How did you do that?" Zintel was asking.

"It's the Sail," I said, exhaustion moving through my limbs. "It, it . . . Everything that ever happened, everyone and everything that ever lived has left an impression. This screen can connect with those impressions."

"Like ghosts?" Zintel asked. There was no vestige of the official left. A deep experience had yanked him by the roots of his mind and he was moved.

"Yes," I said. "I believe so."

"How can that be?"

Joe and the rest of the employees from JTE had gathered around us.

"Their souls are carried, enveloped in another co-existing dimension. These spirits do not dissipate when the body

dies. Vestiges of memory and self-memory live on, kept in place by yet other aspects of an unseen world."

"Horseshit!" Pinkus proclaimed.

No one responded to him.

"How do you know this, Josh?" Joe asked.

Thalla appeared in my mind. It was her touch that gave knowledge, awareness. We had shared something that neither of us realized at the time.

"It was Pinkus," I lied.

"What?" the thin-lipped racist uttered. "I didn't say anything like that."

"Sure you did," I said. "You said that you saw . . . certain images when you were alone with the Sail. I realized that there is a two-way communication between that realm and this—that there's something beckoning to us, calling out beyond what we know."

I could almost feel the hatred coming off the programmer. He despised me more than my girlfriend, Lena Berston, had ever loved me. The intimacy of this revelation sent a mild spasm through my nervous system.

FOR THE NEXT SEVEN HOURS Joe and Ana, Dak and Doreen, and even spiteful Todd Pinkus tested my theory. Cosmo returned after a couple of hours and joined in.

At first we approached the Sail one at a time imagining moments in our lives. This method only worked with Pinkus. Every time he approached the Sail alone it began to show different ways in which children were tortured and

killed. Finally he fled the room, unable to face the demons his presence called forth.

After the general failure of the one-on-Sail approach we tried the interaction method. First Joe stood with his back to the screen like I had and was approached by each of us concentrating on a particular memory. This method only worked when I was the focal point.

Once, when Doreen was remembering a time in her youth when she was the singer for a band, I looked up and saw Thalla watching me from an impossible distance. Her stare was chilly and disapproving.

"I DON'T KNOW what you've got here, Joe," Dak Zintel said that night over pizza and red wine brought in by Cosmo from Pizzaland down the way, "but it's important. I called the head of the defense committee an hour ago and he's sending down a team from the Pentagon."

"Defense?" Doreen said.

"Yes. This is certainly a weapon. It may help us to spy on other countries or interrogate terrorist suspects without them even knowing it. We'll all stay here tonight and tomorrow the military will evaluate the plausibility of the device."

AFTER THAT WE WENT our separate ways within the compound. Zintel said that he'd stay with us and Cosmo promised to work on streamlining the screen for the Sail. Pinkus hadn't been with us since fleeing his monsters and I was disturbed, wandering.

I guess I was waiting for Thalla to show up and advise me, but I had no glimmer of her.

I went to the hangar thinking that proximity to the Sail might summon her, but Cosmo was still there working on the scaffolding above the gossamer weave.

"What you doin', Cos?" I called.

"Just making sure everything's ready for the government," he said. There was an odd tone in his voice, but I ignored it.

That was late at night. I decided to go to Doreen, not for sex but for the comfort of friendship.

I pushed her door open. They didn't see me. Dak Zintel was standing with his pants down around his ankles, while naked and on her knees, Doreen was adoring the congressman's extraordinarily large erection. They were both making moaning sounds that together made a kind of music.

Before either one of them saw me I backed out of the room and closed the door.

ON THE ROOF of our office building I was looking out at the stars, dimmed as they were by the bright lights of L.A.

"How did you do that?" Thalla asked.

I turned and she was standing there beside me, naked as Doreen had been.

"What?" I asked.

"I've been trying to get away from you," she said. "I have used every technique to block our connection. No human has ever overridden an Alto mind."

It was all very clear to me: witnessing the sex between

Doreen and Zintel, added to the sudden acquisition of multidimensional knowledge, had sent an exponential wail through my system. Indeed, my heart was calling out for Thalla; a yearning came from me like a howl from a wolf under the spell of a full moon. Thalla's blue-black eyes saw these thoughts like words written across my face.

I was, as I said, standing in darkness under the late-night L.A. sky. She, wherever she was, stood in bright sunlight.

"You've changed," she said, her tone softening.

"This place you call Soul-matter," I said. "That's where we are. I mean the connection between us."

She smiled and held out a hand.

I flinched away.

"You called to me and now you're afraid?" she said.

"Yes."

"Why?"

"You know why."

"You have never known love."

"I never suspected that it would, it could be like this," I said. "It's in my mind and my past. Our connection is like everything else has been cut loose. I honestly feel that I could float away with the slightest push."

"The rare human that is attuned to Otherworld events is open in ways that few beings can imagine. Even the Alto cannot fully comprehend what you are feeling now."

"Does that mean you don't . . ."

Thalla smiled under that distant sun and I was filled with a feeling that might have killed me a day before.

"We are joined," she said, holding out a hand.

I reached for her. When we touched ecstasy flared from

my spinal column and I think I hollered. Trembling, I fell to my knees. Tears ran down my face and I understood the entire history of religion.

Certain men and women down through the millennia had reached through the veils of existence and delivered unto Man the possibility of purity and the Divine. These prophets and saints, witches and devils touched peoples' hearts the way I touched my fellow workers, the way the Sail touched them.

"It's all right," a man said.

I looked up and found that Cosmo was on his knees, holding me. I tried to speak but my throat clenched down on the words.

"I understand," Cosmo said, and I passed out.

WHEN I CAME BACK to consciousness I was in a bed in a musty room. Images of Christ in dozens of different styles and media adorned the walls. There were paintings and sculptures, frescoes and pages torn from books. Candles flickered at the corners of the room and subtle, roseate incense flavored the air.

I levered up on my elbows and saw Cosmo over by the door. He was sitting in a straight-back wooden chair, leaning against the door and reading what looked like a big, leather-bound Bible.

Cosmo was a lumpy man, going prematurely bald. The hair he had was black with only a few strands of gray, and his eyes were what he called Sicilian green.

I tried to speak but had to clear my throat first.

Looking up Cosmo said, "You're awake."

He smiled and I tried to remember him doing that, smiling at me, but could not conjure the image.

"What happened?" I managed to say.

Cosmo frowned. "You don't remember?"

"Remember what?"

"Mother Mary."

That was the moment my desire to be a playwright fell away. Cosmo was the human comedy, the eternal tragic hero. He embodied the impossibility of understanding and the courage to act, to believe regardless of the limitation.

"She was golden, right?" I said.

"And naked like purity itself," he added. "And rainbow lights flared out of you like a sun right there on the roof, in the middle of the night."

"You saw that?"

Cosmo was wearing cranberry-colored overalls and a long-sleeved cotton shirt decorated with deft drawings of yellow carnations and red poppies.

I suppose I frowned.

"What?" he asked.

"I was just thinking that, aside from a few interviews, you and I have rarely talked."

To my surprise the big peasant fell down on his knees, his head bowed to the floor.

"Forgive," he uttered.

"What?"

"Forgive me."

"I don't understand."

"Spite came from the devil and I hated you," he said.

"Why?"

"I thought black men were evil monkeys that came from Satan to pollute our women and degrade our people."

"Really? You thought that about me?"

"Forgive."

"Please get off your knees, man. It makes me feel very uncomfortable."

He didn't stand but at least he looked up at me.

"When I saw what I saw on the roof I realized that I had been blessed by the presence of a saint. You speak with God. His mother blessed you with her own hand."

I sat up in the bed and patted the place next to me.

"Sit down, Cosmo."

He obeyed averting his eyes.

"I don't know what happened," I said. "I just know that since the Sail has been activated my mind has opened up to things beyond this world."

"Amen," the big Italian said.

"You really hated me for being black?"

"I was wrong."

"I never knew it."

"I'm sorry."

"You don't understand, Cosmo. It's not that I'm angry or even shocked that someone hates another because of race. It's that I didn't know that worries me. It's, it's like this Mother Mary thing you're talking about. Before the Sail I didn't know that we're living in the confluence between many realms. I didn't know that my soul, which I had never believed in, existed on another plane and was immortal along with the souls of dragonflies and synthetic humanity."

Cosmo leaped from the bed and got back down on his knees.

"What now?" I asked.

"I must kneel to hear these words."

"Either sit back down or I won't say anything."

Hesitantly the craftsman got up and sat on the bed. He was a big man but I couldn't even feel the pressure of his weight—he perched so lightly.

"Is government good?" he asked.

"I don't understand."

"That man," Cosmo said, "that Zintel. He's going to turn the Blank Page over to the Pentagon. I do not believe that God was not meant to reside in the halls of politicians."

I understood what he was saying. It wasn't just because of Doreen that I began to have misgivings about Zintel's motives. The idea of the Sail as a weapon was anathema, but I was a law-abiding American citizen. I hadn't even articulated this distrust (and cowardice) to myself.

"He's going to try to use the Blank Page for the rich and powerful, but it belongs to the people," Cosmo said. "Like Jesus does."

I understood the basis of religious fervor, but that didn't make me religious. God, for me, at that moment, was the Intersection between contradictory forms of existence. To Cosmo there was the irrefutable truth of *let there be light*, where my spirituality was more like a child registering the sunrise for the first time in his growing awareness of the world.

None of that mattered. I wasn't going to fight against the government. I wasn't that kind of man.

Cosmo tried to talk to me about resisting Zintel, but I didn't see what we could do.

"Joe owns the Sail and the building," I said. "We're just employees."

"This is more than just some product," Cosmo objected. "The Blank Page is like a leaf of the original scripture. It's the word of God."

What could I say to that? Cosmo was twice as strong as I was and his blind faith was more powerful still.

"I'm going back to my room now," I said. "Let's wait and see how it goes in the morning. We'll hear what the Pentagon folks have to say then."

Cosmo nodded conspiratorially. It was as if he were hearing a whole other set of ideas.

"Yeah," he said. "We'll see what they say and then, if it's blasphemy, we'll know what to do."

"Uh-huh."

"Be ready, my brother," said the man who less than an hour before believed that all I represented was racial pollution.

I LEFT COSMO'S BASEMENT ROOM at two in the morning, wandering over to the hangar. There I found Ana Fried sitting in front of a vast colony of blond monkeys that had made their home by the side of a deep and placid lake. The volume was turned up and the din of the gibbering primates was overpowering.

I touched the chief scientist's shoulder and she turned to me unfazed by my appearance.

"Sorry, Ana," I said. "I missed my post."

"It's okay, Josh," she said. "I want to spend as much time here as I can. Who knows what the government will do tomorrow?"

"Cosmo thinks this is a religious artifact and that anyone working for government is an agent of the devil."

"He's a fanatic and a racist," Ana said. "But he may be right about the good congressman. All I was trying to do was to design a tool, and now they will use it to bring down governments."

"Who knows what they'll do?" I said. "I mean, all we see are beasts."

"Don't help them," Ana said to me.

"What do you mean?"

"They are the ones who carry out the orders of madmen. They built the ovens and the guns and then set them loose on the people."

"But we, we have to do what the government says," I argued.

"The extermination camp guards used that excuse."

I had not seen Ana Fried in this light before. The rest of my time around her she carried the mantle of science like a shield, or maybe a religion. But the entrance of the government had rattled her, too.

She wanted to stay with the Sail and so I left for the office building.

I had almost walked all the way to Doreen's door before I remembered that Zintel was in her room. I went to the second-floor office that I had converted into a bedroom.

Cosmo had brought in mattresses for all of us. I fell

down on mine and was immediately enveloped in a deep sleep.

". . . N𝐨," SHE WAS SAYING, "I cannot bring anything but my essence into your realm."

"But I could feel you," I said.

"What you felt was the transparency of our beings— invisible, intangible, and undeniable."

Thalla and I were sitting across from each other at a rough-hewn stone table on top of a mountain that had no counterpart on my Earth. It soared over a great ocean teeming with life that I knew was there but could not see.

We'd been talking for hours before I woke up. I remembered how, in my reverie, she explained that humanity was like the blind fish that evolved in underground caves.

"Your people have lost the vision and vitality of your ancestors," she said. "Your world consists of licking algae off walls that you bump into quite by accident. Your heavens are dark and unrevealing."

"And cavemen were more sophisticated?" I said, a sneer on my lips.

"So-called primitive man felt the connection and possibilities in the greater world. Through their totems and rare seers they became one with the spirits that live within them, all around them."

"Like ghosts?"

"The human acme of wisdom was the question, 'How many angels can sit on the head of a pin?' This world is crowded into its stratosphere with the spirits and souls of

the physically departed. Humans and insects, fishes of all kinds amid the flickering glitter of trillions upon trillions of single-cell beings."

"Amoebas have souls?"

"Even so-called inert matter has the gleam of the divine in it. Humanity once knew this. But in my world and in yours they have forgotten. Modern man worships anthropomorphic deities rather than the ether of their being."

"But what about technology?" I asked.

"Banging two rocks together and calling the noise science," she said with contempt.

"But, but *I* see it," I said.

"There is power in you," she agreed, "but without the Sail you would have spent your entire life in darkness like those cave fishes."

FULLY AWAKE, I REMEMBERED the question I wanted to ask.

"When the men from the government come today what should I do?"

"What men?"

"Don't you know everything that's happening around me?" I asked.

"No, darling, no. I only see you. The world around is unclear. Unless you're looking right at something the only impression I get are swirling mists."

"But I can see your world—clearly."

"Your abilities are obviously stronger than mine."

I explained about Zintel and Joe. The image of Doreen

and Zintel's sexual romp came unbidden to my mind and I was ashamed.

"Why are you trying to hide your pain?" Thalla asked.

"I guess I feel I shouldn't be jealous now that I know how I feel about you."

"Me?" her smile lit up the surrounding ocean. "I have three husbands. If any of them betrayed me in the way of the Alto I would be devastated and I would bring that pain to you."

"Three husbands?" A question passed through my mind but I tried to squelch it.

"Now and again they serve me together. Alto women have great appetites and little shame. But what needs to happen on your world, in your time, is for you to act on your beliefs."

"About women?"

"About these men trying to appropriate the Sail."

"I don't even know what my beliefs are."

"Then you must discover yourself."

"I can't go against the United States government."

"Why not?"

"They are so much more powerful than I am."

"There is no power anywhere in the megaverse greater than another. This is a truth that the Alto have learned by bitter experience. Even the First Being is only one among the many."

"There is a first being?"

"There is always a first and an again. And if that ideal being is your equal then this thing you call government is nothing . . . less than nothing."

"They could kill me," I argued.

"No," Thalla said, and I took it in as absolute truth.

A door opened in my mind and I understood that who I was, what I was, was immortal. I had existed before my body and would continue on a journey beyond its destruction. I had no proof of this conviction but still it vibrated in my heart.

"Josh," she said.

I felt someone shaking my shoulder.

"Josh."

Doreen was there perched at the edge of my mattress.

"Wake up, honey," she said.

I got a sudden flash of Lena and Ralph rutting on Ralph's couch; the place where I sat so often drinking wine and getting high with my ex-friend. The image was fleeting but it felt different from jealous fantasy. I wasn't jealous and the details seemed . . . real.

"What's wrong?" Doreen asked.

"Nothing. I was just asleep."

"Come on," she said. "Get up. They're waiting for us in the hangar."

"What's the rush?"

"It's ten-thirty."

"What?"

I jumped up off the floor. All I had to do was put on my shoes because I had fallen asleep fully dressed. From there I blundered out into the hall and headed for the stairs.

"Don't you need to brush your teeth or something?" Doreen called after me.

"No. I'm late. Are they already there?"

"Yes."

———

DOREEN'S HIGH HEELS CLICKED and tapped after me as I rushed toward the most important meeting of my life. I could feel my body moving through space; my strength working against gravity. The air was scented with the subtle odor of Doreen's perfume. She had come this way to get me.

As we neared the door to the hangar I felt her hand on my arm.

"Wait," she said.

There was urgency in her clenching fingertips so I stopped and turned. She was wearing a light blue dress-suit with a nacreous blouse underneath. Fashionista as she was, Doreen always had a change of clothes close at hand. Her face was made-up. Only her eyes showed any vulnerability.

I gazed at her fabricated beauty feeling extraordinarily calm.

"Yes, Doreen."

"Did you come into my room last night?"

"I did."

"Did you see, um, Dak?"

Nodding I said, "He's got a really big dick, huh?"

The pain in her face took me by surprise. I was trying to ease the tension by being nonchalant but, like the newborn Alto, I acted when I should have taken things slowly.

"I'm sorry," I said. "I didn't mean—"

"No, I'm sorry," Doreen said. "I didn't realize until I heard the door closing how deeply I felt about you, Josh. But now I see I meant nothing to you."

She hurried past me through the doorway before I could stop her.

I followed. The space before the Sail was unfamiliar to me. There were three extra men (not including Dak Zintel) standing among my cohorts of the past three years.

The men wore dark suits and seemed imposing. The oldest was maybe fifty and the youngest thirty-five, but age was not a factor in their presence. Still, the oldest among them was the senior officer. He was a white man with silver hair that gave the impression of being a natural color sprouting from birth. Of his two aides, one was white and the other black, but, again, their race bore little meaning. They were all around six feet tall and hale in their bearings. I instantly disliked them.

"Josh," Joe Jennings called from the center of the mob.

I took in the expressions of my fellow JTE employees. Ana's face was drawn and wary, Doreen's heart was broken by a pain much deeper than her relationship with me, Joe was open and hopeful, Cosmo's air was indecipherable, and Pinkus looked as if he hadn't slept for days. There were dark rings around his eyes and his thin lips were moving slightly, like dying worms.

"This is him, General Llan," Joe was saying. He walked up and guided me by the arm to the steel-headed blue-eyed representative of the Pentagon.

"Pleased to meet you," I said, wondering where those words came from in the field of my mind.

"Mr. Winterland," General Llan said. "I hear that you have a certain rapport with this device."

"So it seems," I said.

"Would you like to show us?"

Everyone in the room was looking at me.

"On one condition," I said.

"What's that?"

I turned my gaze to Doreen and said, "If you promise to have a private conversation with me right after the test is over."

"Josh," she said, chiding me with her tone.

"That's my one condition."

I had seen passion in Doreen's face before but never had I witnessed that scarlet hue rise under her skin. She looked down and away, but when she turned back again I was still there.

"All right," she said. "I talk to you all the time anyway."

"Give me your hand, General," I said then.

"What?"

"I said . . . give me your hand."

"Is this part of the condition or the test?"

Instead of answering I held out my right hand.

It was a pleasure to see the discomfiture in the Washingtonian's face. I hated him and his aides at first sight, their arrogant bearing and military pomposity.

He took my hand as if he was going to shake it again but I didn't allow him to go through with the motion.

"Tell me about your mother," I commanded.

"What?" he said, but it was already too late.

On the Sail a woman appeared as seen through a nearly closed door. She was naked, leaning up against a kitchen table with an adolescent boy on his knees in front of her.

Her orgasm was something more than I had ever experienced. The reed-thin teenager stood up exhibiting an equally slender erection. The woman leered at what her nakedness had wrought.

General Llan blanched under the image. He jerked his hand away and yelled, "Turn that off!"

"It's not *on*, sir," I said. "For the past few days the Sail has been powered only by the sun filtering in from the skylight or, at night, from the lamps."

"I said turn it off!" he hollered.

He grabbed me by my wrinkled shirt and I allowed myself to be swung around.

"We don't know how to turn it off, General," I said.

By this time Joe was lowering the screen that Cosmo had built.

"Don't you see," Pinkus said under labored breath. "It's an abomination. It should be destroyed."

The ragged pain in the programmer's voice demanded attention. He was standing at an odd angle as if there was a spasm twisting his spine. When he spoke spit leaped from his mouth.

"It finds evil and throws it at you. It's, it's a devil in there. It wants to crush everything good in the world. I feel it. I feel it calling to me in the night. There are men on top of boys, women with knives getting their revenge on babies. There's blood . . ."

Pinkus fell to his knees blubbering so uncontrollably that the rest of his diatribe was lost to us.

Doreen hurried over and knelt down, taking the broken man into her arms.

In the meantime General Llan was on his cell phone, muttering.

Soon after the door to the outside opened and two armed soldiers in fancy dress uniform entered. One was a man and the other a woman. They were young and intent.

"Marley, Thringold," the general said. "These people are to be kept here until I return. Secure them in a holding area and keep them there until we return."

The man saluted while the woman leveled her rifle at us.

"What is this?" Ana Fried demanded.

"If anyone tries to escape," the general said, "deadly force is authorized."

"Sir, yes, sir," the man-soldier said.

I wondered how often the general had seen the woman and the paperboy or teenaged gardener. Was it his mother or some other caretaker? Had the Sail registered the memory or had it somehow found the woman's soul and dragged it back to relive the future soldier's torment?

"Move it," the man-soldier ordered.

WE WERE TAKEN to the subterranean shower room beneath the hangar. Joe had told Zintel where it was. The congressman was not under arrest. In his defense, he tried to get the general to leave us under our own cognizance, but that idea was shot down. Then Dak tried to get Joe released into his custody, but one of the aides talked the general out of that.

We were trundled down the metal stairs into the hollowed-out concrete cube that had three wooden stalls

for showers and two long redwood benches. There were no windows and only one door. The soldiers sat outside guarding us, imprisoning us.

"I can't believe this," Joe Jennings said. "I just can't."

I thought this crisis of belief was brought on because they kept him down with us. After all, he was a rich man who owned the property that so frightened the general.

"Believe it," Ana Fried said. "They would kill each and every one of us if they believed we were a threat to their dominance."

"They're trying to protect the people, Ana," Joe said.

"Are we not the people?" the scientist asked.

For the most part the rest of us were quiet. No one knew how long we'd be there or where the general had gone.

Pinkus sat hugging his knees on the floor in the far corner, mumbling to himself and nodding now and again. The Sail had taken its toll on him.

After maybe an hour Doreen sidled up beside me.

"Well?" she asked.

"What?"

"You said you wanted to say something to me?"

I gazed into Doreen's walnut-colored eyes, remembering all the years I had been bereft and never known it, all the love I'd missed and the life I hadn't lived.

"Well?" she asked again.

"I misspoke before. I wanted to put you at ease, to say that I wasn't angry. Instead I came off as cold, diffident. I want you in my life, Doreen."

I could see the shift in her body language. She leaned toward me and exhaled through her nostrils.

"I don't know what it is about me and sex, Josh. I mean, I've slept with so many men, and women, too, but I don't know why. Sometimes it feels like it's not even me. I usually don't know what I feel about someone until long after the relationship or one-night stand is over."

She kissed me and then stared into my face.

"You're different," she said.

I'd heard those words before . . . from Thalla when last we met. Where was Thalla? Would I see her again?

She kissed me again and then drifted away toward poor Pinkus. He was drooling steadily by then.

"Sir," Cosmo said. He'd been waiting for Doreen to leave my side.

"Come on, Cos, call me Josh."

"I've taken care of everything."

"What do you mean?"

"I am your soldier, like those outside the door. I serve you like they serve evil. I would die for you, sir. That is my meaning on Earth."

"No one's gonna die, Cosmo."

"I am ready to die . . . for you."

He grabbed my left shoulder and squeezed. Cosmo was a powerful man. I had to grind my teeth to endure the pain of his adoration.

HOURS PASSED. AT ONE POINT, after Doreen had been cradling Pinkus for some time, he stood up and pushed her away.

"Get away from me, harlot!" he yelled.

Doreen fell to the floor and Cosmo clocked Pinkus. The madman fell to the floor ranting and bleeding from a cut on his forehead.

"Cunts and bitches! Pimps and thieves! Little demons that claw me raw and feast on the meat of my genitals!"

He said more and I wished that I hadn't understood him. But as he spoke I glimpsed transparent images of the demons that assailed Pinkus. He was a living man in this *inert* dimension, but he was also connected to a vast plane of suffering and carnal desires thirsting for blood and rape and death over and over.

I was nearly overcome by the pain he experienced. The Sail had brought this out in him but it had always been there.

No wonder Man had moved away from Knowledge.

NOT LONG AFTER PINKUS'S outbreak General Llan returned. His aides were not in evidence but the soldiers were with him, leveling their semiautomatic rifles at us.

We were, I imagined, moments away from death.

"I have conferred with the Joint Chiefs of Staff and the president," Llan said. "They agree with me that this device, this artifact, is too dangerous to be left to the open market."

"This property is mine, General," Joe said. He took a step forward to indicate his rights and his willingness to fight for them.

"The screen and all of you will be brought to Washington," Llan told Jennings. "This is a matter of national security and falls under the province of the Patriot Act."

I was stuck on the idea of the Sail being anyone's property. The notion was ridiculous. It would be like a small-
town bank claiming ownership of the air we breathe.

"You can't do this," Joe Jennings said.

"You called them," Ana told our boss.

He turned to her, a look of utter confusion on his face. A
lifetime of self-certainty and an ironclad belief system had
fallen apart for Joe.

"Gather them up and bring them with us," the general
said to his soldiers.

MAYBE IF WE had been criminals we would have stood up
against the injustice of our captors. But as it was we were
chattel. Ana, Doreen, Joe, myself, and even Cosmo showed
his hands when ordered to and filed up the stainless-steel
stairs. The man-soldier forced Pinkus to his feet and kept
him aloft by the arm while still pointing his rifle at us.

They herded us back under the covered Sail. Two other
soldiers, one of them on a tall ladder, were trying to work
the mechanism that Cosmo jury-rigged to cover the sacred
mechanism.

"General," the man-soldier on the ladder said.

"Tyler," Llan replied.

"We can't get the screen off, and that's keeping us away
from the device itself. Do you want us to break it?"

"If you do that you'll tear the sheet," Cosmo said. "The
screen gets stuck sometimes. Let me get up there and I can
fix it."

The general turned his dominant gaze upon the fanatic

Italian. Their eyes met in what I imagined to be an unwanted, unrealized kinship.

"All right," the general said. "Tyler."

"Yes, sir."

"Get down from there and let this man do his job."

I remember every word spoken because, later on, they all seemed so prophetic. I was partially aware of all the intersecting dimensions around us and the various mental dimensions among us in that room.

What I didn't remember was any problem with the screen sticking.

Cosmo went through a few workman-like motions and then called down, "It'll work now, Tyler."

That was when what I call the Final Dance began.

"Don't raise the screen," Pinkus said. But no one responded.

Cosmo moved down the ladder with accomplished crab-like movements while Tyler's partner turned the little wheel designed to work the covering screen.

"This is my property, General," Joe was saying. But no one cared about him, either.

The scene being revealed on the Sail was from the minute point of view of a dark red ant among thousands of its hive members marching up the side of a towering tree. There was no sound but I could almost feel the vibrations coming from the ants. I wondered if this experience was a communication between this world and the next. Was the Sail translating the memories of ants so that I could glean some small part of their high adventure?

Suddenly, as if called up by the fervor of the ants, a flame

started at the bottom of the Sail. Quickly the fire rose to
envelop the entire scene. I gasped and grabbed at my heart
like a bad actor in an old silent movie.

"Yes! Burn it down! Yes!" Pinkus cried.

I was so bereft by the destruction of the Sail that I paid
no attention to Pinkus's screams until the deafening report.

I jerked my head toward the soldier supporting Pinkus. I
worried that the distraught programmer had done something to get himself shot. But instead I saw that it was the
soldier who had been gunned down by his own pistol.
Pinkus had pulled the weapon from its holster; he'd shot
the soldier and was now firing at the rest of us under the
burning screen.

The general was hit, then Doreen, then the woman soldier. I fell to the ground and rolled up into a ball—not the
wisest of moves.

"Motherfucker!" Pinkus yelled.

I looked up and there he was pointing the pistol at my
head.

There was a masculine scream, more like a roar, and then
Cosmo was on Pinkus, his craftsman's hands around the
programmer's throat. Three shots were fired and both men
fell in a heap.

I tried to get up but a soldier, I think it was Tyler,
shouted, "Stay on the ground and keep your hands where I
can see them!"

The odor of gunpowder underlain by the tangy scent of
spilled blood assailed my nostrils, but I stayed on the
ground thinking about the intersecting dimensions of Man
and more . . .

GENERAL LLAN WAS HIT in the shoulder and was back on duty seven days after the shooting. Joe Jennings was shot in the thigh. He took three months off and then went to work on a government project to re-create the Sail for military purposes. I suppose his first hire would have been Ana Fried, but she had a nervous breakdown after the incident and has never completely recovered. Cosmo and Pinkus died in their deadly embrace; Pinkus of a broken neck and Cosmo due to massive internal bleeding and organ damage.

Doreen was shot through the heart and died instantly. I often think of her and the two dead soldiers (Marley and Thringold, I never knew which was which).

Cosmo had set a bottle of some kind of accelerant at the top of the Sail. The liquid caught fire upon drying. When he went up to free the screen mechanism (which he had jammed), he opened the bottle and the accelerant started dripping down. I found all this out later, during my time in military custody.

I was arrested and questioned for over ninety hours without a break.

"All I did was keep the records," I told them over and over again. "Notebooks and videos. They're all in the office."

"Did you know that Mr. Compabasso planned to burn Mr. Jennings's property?" a dozen different men asked me.

"No."

"Did you know that Mr. Pinkus was homicidal?"

"Not until he was."

I WAS KEPT imprisoned for four months in a small gray room on an army base somewhere south of L.A. At the end of that time I was brought before a military and civilian court where I was told that the information I had was vital to national security. I was warned that if I divulged that information I could be imprisoned for an indeterminate period of time under the National Security Act of 1948. After the hearing I signed papers for half an hour and was given bus fare to L.A.

There I found that I had been evicted and that my belongings had been discarded. I couldn't tell the property manager that I was in military jail because one of the dozens of documents I signed forbade me to say anything that might even refer to the project I had been working on.

I slept at a homeless shelter downtown for three days until I finally got a phone number for Joe Jennings's new company—Microfibers Inc.

Joe said that he couldn't hire me and that he couldn't tell me why he couldn't but I already knew; he probably signed the same papers I had. He did wire me my settlement check—three months wages.

WHEN I GOT to my mother's house in Oakland there was no one home.

The front and back doors were locked as were all the windows. I finally had to break in through the glass to clamber into my childhood bedroom. The house was very

neat and somehow seemed unlived-in. The sink was empty and my mother's bed was covered with only the fitted sheet.

It was two o'clock in the afternoon. My mother, Ida Lathea Mackie-Winterland, was always home at that time watching her afternoon talk shows.

I went to the small kitchen and poured water from the faucet into a red plastic tumbler—my favorite glass when I was a child. I was looking through the window over the sink at the withered oak in our backyard when there came a knock.

I went to the door and opened it. Why not? It was my mother's home after all.

Three policemen and one policewoman had their pistols pointed at my head.

"On the ground," one of them said in an almost pleasant tone.

My experiences over the past months had prepared me for the militarism of the American legal system. I lowered to my knees, placed the cup gently on the floor, and then got down on my belly with my arms stretched out over my head. Someone jerked my hands back and secured them with a plastic tie. The sure-footed officers of the law passed by me into the house looking for corpses or state secrets.

"Please leave the area," an official voice said.

"Fine, Officer," a woman replied. I recognized the tones but forgot the name and even the face. "But first you tell me why you are arresting a man for bein' in his own house."

"This is a burglar, ma'am," the policeman said.

"I've known Joshua Winterland since he was a baby swaddled in cotton blankets, Officer," Lonnie Brighthome

replied. "If he's a burglar then I'm Jack the Ripper to boot."

"He was seen breaking in a window," the official countered.

"His window," my mother's best friend corrected.

THIS DISCUSSION WENT ON for some time while I laid there on the inner threshold of my family home. The police demanded Mrs. Brighthome's identification and then they rifled through my pants for mine.

"Where is his mother?" the woman cop asked Lonnie.

"Am I her keeper?" the elderly black woman replied.

Finally I was brought to my feet and released.

"Next time, call the police when you have a problem," the senior cop told me. They were preparing to leave.

I looked at the tall, balding black officer wondering what he meant exactly. The next time I returned home after almost being murdered and then jailed for the privilege, on that next time should I call the police if I found the door to my own house locked?

I didn't say those words. I didn't say anything. There was a familiar and yet strange buzz tickling the base of my skull and a sharp pain in my left shoulder from the way the police had bent my arm.

AFTER THE POLICE LEFT Lonnie Brighthome came in and sat by my side on my mother's sofa. She took my hands and stared into my eyes.

Lonnie was thin and dark-skinned, maybe seventy years old. I remembered her as being tall, but that was through a child's eyes. Her face seemed different.

"Didn't you use to wear glasses, Mrs. Brighthome?"

"Your mother died Sunday last."

THERE'S A CERTAIN REDUNDANCY to the day or so after I learned of my mother's death. She had a stroke while praying in church on a Wednesday evening when no one else was around. Peter Flim, long-time church janitor, found her the next morning, still bowing, nearly dead.

I cried and thrashed around, slept on the couch because I was afraid of my mother's room and mine. I called old friends and had long talks and cried more. I was the only child of a single mother and now alone in the world.

My mother had been alone because I was taken away under the blanket of national security. I began to hate the power exerted over my physical body by government agents who never even apologized.

IT WASN'T UNTIL my third night home that I went into my room. I hadn't returned since breaking the windowpane.

I lay down on the slender bed surrounded by posters from plays that I'd collected since puberty.

The phone rang. There was an extension in my room and so I didn't even have to sit up to answer.

"Hello?"

"Josh?"

"Lena?"

"Nathan called me," she said. "He told me that your mother had died."

I didn't say anything. She hadn't asked a question.

"How are you, Josh?"

"I don't know. My life seems kind of off." I laughed as if to prove the point.

"What happened?"

"To my mother?"

"Yes."

"A stroke."

"You could have asked me to come to the funeral."

"I was out of town."

"Where?"

I saw something out of the corner of my eye and there she was—Thalla sitting on a satin stool under a clear roof revealing an aquamarine sea.

"I have to go, Lena."

"But I, I wanted to talk to you," she said. "About what happened."

"I'll call you later."

"When."

"I don't know," I said and then I hung up.

Thalla turned to me and smiled.

"I thought your body had died," she said.

I rushed toward her and placed my hand on the image of her face. The resultant ecstasy was more than sex could ever be. It was what they write about in popular songs and sacred texts—touching souls.

WHEN I CAME BACK to consciousness she was sitting on the floor of her suboceanic abode, next to me and a universe (or two) away.

"How are your husbands?" was my first question.

"Score-ti is dead," she said sadly. "Killed in the war."

"What war?"

"Do you remember Father Time?"

"The machine that contained a hundred million human minds?"

"After two centuries Refuge has decided that the Alto are a threat to their existence. They have been attacking us."

"Are they more powerful than you?"

"No. But we are hesitant to use our most destructive weapons against them. Their rage at us is valid. We did slaughter their species after all."

"I don't want you to die, Thalla."

"I thought you were dead," she said. "Long evenings I would sit by my globes hoping that you would call to me."

I explained how Cosmo burned the Sail.

"But if it is destroyed how can you contact me?" she asked.

"I never used the Sail to contact you."

"But you were attuned to it," she said. "The vibrations from the Sail made it possible for us to communicate."

"And if it was destroyed?"

"Our contact should be impossible."

We talked for hours about the war and my incarceration; about the impossibility of our communication and the

depth of feeling that still linked us. Now and again we'd touch, feeling that connection denied to physical beings.

"Is this how Cosmo and Doreen feel all the time?" I asked my platonic lover.

"Yes."

"And Pinkus, too?"

"There is no heaven or hell, Josh, Joshua."

"Could I contact my mother?"

"Not without the Sail."

THE NEXT MORNING I noticed a brown paper package next to my dresser. It had fallen down, possibly when neighbors were searching my room, trying to find out how to contact me.

There was no return address but the postmark was from more than three months earlier.

When I opened the package I was stunned to see a smaller version of the Sail. It was three feet by two, rife with vibrating colors that I knew were striving to come to life.

There was a note attached, written in a bold hand.

Dear Josh,

I'm writing this to you after seeing the Vision of Mother Mary.

When I started working for JTE, weaving the Blank Page, I also started bringing home strands of the fabric to practice with. I built a loom and went over the process I'd use at work. I didn't know why at the time but I

kept this a secret. Now I realize that the piece I've woven
was meant for you. Tomorrow I will destroy the Page at
work and you will receive this package from your
mother. Take it and do what you think best.

Cosmo

I hugged the fabric to my chest and face. Thalla was there
instantly, in my arms, almost real.

Her shock and delight were obvious. I rubbed my lips on
the Sail and she closed her eyes in sensual pleasure.

"Joshua."

"Yes."

"You can't just grab me out of time like that. What if I
were with one of my husbands, or worse, in battle?"

"I just grabbed the thing when I saw it," I said. "I didn't
know it would connect to you . . . like this."

She was a woman in my arms pulsing with a life force
stronger than any human.

"We are attuned to each other, Joshua. In this life and
the next our souls shall always be drawn together."

"Your husbands don't know about me?"

"No." She didn't need to say anything else.

THE NEXT FEW MONTHS were sublime and limitless.
Thalla was with me during most of the waking hours of
every day. We talked and communed. She taught me how to
make a deeper connection with the Sail; how to speak to it
and how to enter its dance. I stood upon Paleolithic plains
and swam among huge sharks in the prehistoric seas of

Earth. I actually flew through the skies with predators and hummingbirds, winged lizards and swarms of bees.

"How can there be room for every life that has ever lived?" I asked maybe three weeks after I'd found her again.

"How many angels can fit on the head of a pin?" she replied.

"Every human?" I asked.

"And more."

"Birds and flies and viruses?"

"And that is only the beginning."

"What else can there be?"

"Alien life forms," she said. "Breathing mountains and fire that minds itself; unique manifestations of consciousness and even the heart of black holes scintillated by unaffected streams of dark matter.

"There is so much life in the next world that it makes our sterile existence akin to the barrenness of space by comparison."

"Aliens?" I said softly. "Murderers and rapists and . . . and . . ."

"All," she said. Then she touched me with her lips and I didn't care.

I WAS WITH THALLA when giant underwater ships attacked her oceanic lair. They were the size of small cities sending barrages of depth charges and torpedoes at the seemingly sheer glass protecting the small colony of Alto.

Thalla's people responded with weapons that sent out rainbow-like rays at the monolithic machines. These weap-

ons seemed to have no effect on the attackers. I said this to Thalla.

"These are specially designed radiations that are aging certain metals that hold the ships together," she told me. "After a while the living machines inside the shells will have to leave for the surface because we are too deep for them to survive the crushing atmosphere."

"Then what?"

"We will seek a new home. We will hide until they find us again."

"And the same thing will happen?"

"By then they will have solved the problem of our accelerated time rays and we will have developed another defensive device."

"What if they find ways around all your defenses?"

Thalla reached out almost touching my face. Then she withdrew the hand.

"The residents of the Crystal City have decided to reclaim their humanity. They have the DNA structures and have been experimenting with synthetic humans such as ourselves. So far these experiments have been failures.

"The humans inside the machines worry that if they regain their corporeal selves that we will attempt to destroy them again. They remember the dying of humanity and the way we ripped them from their bodies.

"But our philosophers believe that this war will hone an attitude toward us that will end in a treaty where the humans will no longer try to destroy us and we, human and Alto, will be able to live in peace."

"But you don't believe that," I said with conviction.

"The humans stored in Father Time will never regain the humanity they once knew. They are now only faulty memories of what they once were."

"You destroyed their souls?"

"No. We severed their memories from their connection to their humanity."

"That's like killing God," I said.

"The war will go on," Thalla averred. "The memory of humanity will finally make machines so big and so powerful that we will not be able to resist. We'll have to escape this world."

"But you said that you could destroy these machines."

"None of us have the heart to destroy humanity again."

"Then come here," I said. "Come to me. Come to my Earth."

The blue-black of Thalla's eyes made me forget the battle raging outside her windows.

"But we committed genocide on your race," she said.

"But you've realized that you were wrong."

"Our scientists have speculated that the strongest emotion in the human breast is the desire for revenge. This is why your species has survived for so long."

"Come to me," I said again, and for the first time I saw an Alto cry.

TIME PASSED. THALLA MET with her people and they began the long parliament on the proposed egress from their Earth. This meeting would take at least seven years she told me. After that they would have to concentrate their great

communal intelligence on how to navigate the dimension in order to leave one home for another.

I was designated as the representative of Earth. I would make up the rules and set out the limitations that would govern the relationship between Alto and human.

I suppose that this was a great responsibility but I didn't feel the weight. I was in love with Thalla and would have done anything to have her in my arms.

Once a day for fifteen minutes that felt like a dozen years I stood in the Golden Chamber of the Alto, a hundred miles beneath the Gobi Desert. Above, huge machines steered by the remnants of remembered humanity searched for us.

The content of these meetings was obscure, abstract, and indecipherable in all but the most esoteric human terms. I would try to describe it here, but other problems arose that drew me away from the Alto's Exodus Hearings.

I KEPT COSMO'S miniature Sail with me at all times. I slept with it and carried it around in a leather satchel whenever I went anywhere—even if only from the bedroom to the kitchen. That thin weave of synthetic fabric meant more to me than anything or anyone in my mortal life. If I went to the store or on a rare trip to the bank I carried the Sail with me.

So on one Thursday when there was no food in the house I trundled up my magic sheet and walked six blocks to a small supermarket where I bought four cans of tomato soup and a five-pound bag of white rice. My mother had left a bank account with sixty-two hundred dollars in it. I was a

signatory on that account and so could survive for at least a while without working.

I was walking home half in this world and half in the Golden Chamber listening to words I had spoken into a dream.

Half a block from my mother's house I saw six black cars parked on the sidewalk, in the driveway, and even on my mother's lawn.

Men and women in suits and uniforms milled around like ants invading a rival hive.

The memory of those four days of questioning and the small gray room where I didn't even have a book came back to me. The Sail in my satchel wailed in my mind and I turned away.

SIX YEARS LATER, after changing my name to Herald Riley, I'm living in New York City; in a one-bedroom apartment on a block that's still inhabited by mostly working-class black people. I make my living as a therapist. The couch my patients lay upon is undergirded by the Sail. They lie back and I can see into their conflicts and miseries, their crimes and losses. No one lies to me on that couch. They pay twenty dollars a session and I have never had a dissatisfied customer.

I have a girlfriend named Dolores and my life-mate Thalla who lives further away than Mercury could run in a god's lifetime.

The government is looking for me, I'm sure. The Alto are settling the finer points to their migration to Earth.

Sometimes at night I dream that Thalla's people see my world and decide to destroy my people. I imagine the loneliness and desolation of an entire species rendered barren. But I wake up to the conviction of saving my beloved's race.

At night I hang up the Sail and talk to my mother and Cosmo, Abraham Lincoln and John Wilkes Booth, to the young huntress of the early reptilian race. And in the morning I see my fellow human beings like children thinking that all the world is close at hand.